AN EVANS NOVEL OF THE WEST

DOS CABALLOS

HUGH ZACHARY

M. EVANS & COMPANY, INC.   NEW YORK

Library of Congress Cataloging-in-Publication Data

Zachary, Hugh

  Dos caballos / Hugh Zachary.
    p.   cm. — (An Evans novel of the west)
  ISBN 0-87131-577-7
  I. Series.
PS3576.A23D6 1989 89-34172
813'.54—dc20

M. Evans and Company, Inc.
216 East 49 Street
New York, New York 10017

Manufactured in the United States of America

9 8 7 6 5 4 3 2 1

Chapter One

The pleasant nip in the early-morning air gave old Jughead illusions of youth and friskiness. "Now you just simmer down," Lucky Smith told the horse as he slung the battered saddle atop the blanket and cinched it in. The black mule named Coaly—Lucky had never been a truly imaginative man when it came to names—was as lackadaisical as ever. It was almost as if he realized that he wouldn't be burdened with anything more than Lucky's bedroll and cooking gear for the trip down the hill.

Lamplight glowed through the windows of a couple of the adobe houses that—along with the general store, the cantina, and Lucky's stable and blacksmith shop—formed the village of Dos Caballos in the Fray Cristobal Mountains. It was a place that could never, because of its name, be called a one-horse town. There was no activity on the streets, nor at the general store that was operated at a great profit mostly by Zelma Clemmons, while her husband, Mack, was roaming the arid hills looking for the mother lode.

Old Jughead broke wind in a series of rumbling explosions as the little caravan passed the cantina and angled toward the trail alongside the creek. The trail began to climb as the canyon narrowed. The sun came up as Lucky passed the rapids, warming his neck and causing diamonds to sparkle in the white water. He leaned back in the saddle, squinted up

1

at the sun. It was going to be another brilliant, sun-saturated day. He slumped comfortably, thinking about how he'd spend one night in the mountains and then pitch camp on the banks of the Rio Grande on the second night. That made him think of Maddy and how they'd slept under the stars on the bank of the river on the way into the mountains. He thought about Maddy a lot, and it was always painful because it had been his bad luck—no, his stupidity—that had killed her, along with the boy who hadn't stayed in the world long enough for his father to get to know him.

Off to the south, a circling of buzzards indicated what might have been the remnants of the kill of a mountain cat. The sun was warming the air quickly. Lucky removed his sheepskin coat and secured it behind the saddle, pushed back his hat, examined the trail ahead with squinted, steel-gray eyes. Jughead was old, but he had an easy, relaxed walking pace that allowed a man to doze a bit as morning became noon and the sun burned down from directly overhead. Between dozing and wakeful dreaming, he let the old horse pick the way. He was seeing two female faces in his mind: his dead wife, Maddy; and the very much alive daughter of the owner of the Dos Caballos Cantina, Catalina Carranza.

Behind him, Coaly's hoof slipped on a rock and the stone clattered down over a sheer drop, gathering others as it rolled to crash dustily into the brush far below. Lucky came alert, looked around, slumped again.

"Maddy," he said aloud, "I reckon you might think I'm fickle, what with it only being three years. You know, Maddy, that I wouldn't be thinking like this if you were alive, but I guess you know also, being that you were quite a woman, how I feel. Now, I know Catalina is young, and maybe you're thinking that I'm just an old duffer and that those mule kicks have addled me, I don't know."

Lucky really did feel that Maddy would understand his feelings for the dark-eyed Catalina, and might even approve. After all, he was twenty-eight, and although men died before and at that age in New Mexico, he was in good shape and the air at Dos Caballos was healthy. He felt good enough to live to be a hundred, and he didn't want to do that much time alone.

In the hottest part of the day, with Lucky slumped in the saddle mixing dozing with dreaming, old Jughead picked his way gingerly up a steep switchback. Lucky was enjoying the solitude. He felt pretty good about being the only white man in the hills west of Dos Caballos.

A road runner dashed out of the rocks uphill from the road. Jughead, startled, snorted. Lucky came awake. He removed his hat and slung sweat off his forehead with his forefinger. He looked around and had a feeling of disorientation. The road was nothing more than a weathering, narrow ledge cut into the side of a steep slope. The hill towered over him and the slope dropped at a steep angle into a dry canyon. A couple of hundred feet ahead, the road disappeared under an old rock slide.

"Doggone you, Jughead," Lucky said, unable to spot one landmark. "You know the way down this dad-gummed hill, and look where you've brought us."

The road had become so narrow that it was going to be tricky getting Coaly turned around. Lucky dismounted and talked soothingly to the mule, who didn't like the idea of hanging his head out over the drop. The contest of will made the sweat pop out through Lucky's shirt. He had a great idea and turned Coaly the other way, with his head toward the high side of the road. Soon the mule's head was pointing back down the road and Lucky performed the same deed with Jughead. He got out front to lead Coaly until the trail widened enough to allow Jughead to get past. Down on the canyon bottom, sunlight glinted off a reflective surface. He didn't give it much attention, except to think idly that the sun had reflected off a quartz rock. He took a couple of steps and the light hit him in the eyes, too bright, too intense to be just the reflection off a chunk of quartz.

He had a debate with himself. It was a long way down, and it would be rough going through dry brush and cactus. He said, "All right, boys, let's go," and started walking. He stopped suddenly, and Coaly jammed his big black head into his back. He looked down into the dry canyon, sighed, resigned himself to the climb as punishment for his curiosity. He secured both sets of reins to protruding rocks and started looking for a way down.

His luck held. He wasn't ten feet below the road before his foot turned on a loose rock and he tumbled for an eternity, coming to rest on a sandy ledge. He had a few bruises and some prickly-pear thorns in his thigh. He dusted himself off, pulled out the cactus spines, and was tempted to restore words to his vocabulary that he'd given up when he married a preacher's daughter back in Kansas. He was more careful as he negotiated the remaining distance to the canyon bottom and began to pick his way through the brush toward the location of the sun flashes. Then he saw the gleam of cracking varnish on polished wood.

To reach the wreckage on the floor of the canyon, he had to push his way through dense brush and past the skeletons of at least two horses, maybe more. The bones were well gnawed by coyotes, bleached white by the sun, and so intermixed that it would have taken a horse doctor to tell just how many animals had died. He bent and picked up a rusted piece of metal, a harness link. He suspected that coyotes would have eaten the harness. Then he walked around the wreck, flicking sweat from his forehead with his forefinger. He recognized the wreckage for what it was: a Concord coach.

The barn-red body had been severely damaged by the fall from the road above, but the yellow paint on the running gear was still brilliant. On the one exposed door there was a faded, fanciful landscape of tall mountains, a lake, pine trees. The ornate scrollwork on the lower panel of the coach's side was right pretty, Lucky thought. Two wheels, one front and one rear, had smashed spokes. The iron rim of one wheel was bent. Lucky looked up the road high above and imagined how it must have happened. The two portside wheels must have slipped over the edge of the road. There would have been no one around to see the crash or to hear the panicked screams of the horses as they were dragged over the drop by the weight of the coach. He wondered if people had died as the stage rolled and rumbled down the mountainside. He saw only the bones of dead horses as he removed his hat and looked around, scratching his head. He was thinking that he could use the iron from the rims in the blacksmith shop. The brass fittings were corroded but could be polished up nicely. The wood of the coach was still solid, keeping well in the dry desert air.

He plundered through the wreckage and found nothing of real value, but he was intrigued. He decided that he'd come back when he had the time, and he had plenty of that, to salvage anything usable. Maybe he could borrow Osa's wagon and even haul back the lower panels of the coach's side with the pretty scrollwork.

Jughead found his way to the Rio Grande with a minimum of guidance from Lucky, and man and animals drank deeply and cavorted—at least Lucky did; the animals were dignified—naked in the water. Lucky dined regally on beans and coffee boiled with Rio Grande water and went to sleep thinking about Catalina.

By the time he reached his destination, upstream at Socorro, Lucky was dry for something more enjoyable than water, and Socorro was well equipped to supply that need. After he'd rubbed down both the bony flanks of Jughead and the sleek, black hide of old Coaly and turned them loose in the stable corral, he dusted his way up the street to Socorro's finest watering spot. It was by that time late afternoon, and since the residents of New Mexico Territory didn't care too much whether the sun was over the yardarm or not, the saloon was crowded. Lucky found a spot at the bar and savored a shot of whiskey that was a bit more mellow than what Osa served at the Dos Caballos. He recognized a couple of men, one of them standing with his back half turned to Lucky, a man nearing middle age who had a thinning head of graying hair but still was in excellent shape.

"Afternoon, Mr. Wilson," Lucky said.

Chunk Wilson turned one well-tailored shoulder slightly toward Lucky and grunted a greeting, then returned to his conversation.

Lucky couldn't help overhearing. Chunk Wilson and the others were talking about the discontinuance of stage service by the Overland Stage Company. It was rumored that the southwestern routes were to be abandoned in favor of the more direct track to California through Salt Lake City. The drinking citizens of Socorro had explicit words to describe the ancestry of those who had made the decision, up to and including John Butterfield and his partners, and the new owners of the Overland Mail. One drinker expressed a profane prayer that all the coaches would sink up to their windows in the snows of Colorado.

Lucky's interest in the conversation was heightened when it became apparent that Chunk Wilson had not been content to let stage service in New Mexico die. He had bought surplus horses and equipment, including the change stations, wells, corrals, blacksmith shops and mules, a few coaches and some stage wagons, and was going to keep service going between El Paso and Sante Fe, with plans to connect farther west, to Arizona, in the near future.

"Say," Lucky said, "that's real smart of you, Mr. Wilson. Makes me real proud."

"Thank you," Wilson grunted.

Lucky finished his drink, motioned for a refill, thinking all the while. "Mr. Wilson," he said when he found an opening in the conversation from which he had been excluded.

Wilson turned. His eyes were surprisingly warm, in direct contrast to his stern face and his drooping mustache.

"I think it would be real nice if you could see fit to make a spur run up to Dos Caballos now and then," Lucky said.

Behind Wilson, a man laughed. Lucky knew the man only by sight and by name, one of Wilson's men, one Craw Maddock. Word was that he was quick with the new wonder he wore strapped in its holster low on his right hip, Colt's newest revolver, the .44-caliber Army 1860. When Lucky made his helpful suggestion to Chunk Wilson regarding stage service to Dos Caballos, he didn't know about Craw Maddock's new wonder revolver. Lucky didn't study guns much. His old Colt Navy Model 1851 was in his saddlebags in case he had to shoot a rattlesnake, and he tried for a deer now and then with a Sharps breechloader, his only inheritance from his father.

"Well, I just thought," Lucky said, "being as how we all have to pack in everything—"

"This here desert rat," Craw Maddock said, "thinks alls Mr. Wilson got to do is carry beans up into them hills." His laugh was echoed by others. Lucky turned back to the bar, his face expressionless.

Craw Maddock had earned his reputation. He had a mean, thin, hungry-looking face and odd, colorless eyes. He affected black, to go with his reputation of having killed at least a dozen men, one of them simply because the man had felt the call of nature in the middle of the night while sleeping in the same room with Craw in a boardinghouse in Portales and woke Craw. Life in the raw, sparsely populated territory of New Mexico suited Craw well. In the absence of organized law enforcement, he was his own law.

"Hey, dust eater," Craw said, "you got any more of them fine-feathered suggestions for Mr. Wilson?"

Wilson had moved away from the bar so that there was no one between Maddock and Lucky. Lucky looked up, a little grin on his face, but with squinted, cold gray eyes. "Don't see no cause for unfriendliness, Maddock," he said. "I was just entering into what I thought was a friendly conversation."

"I didn't hear nobody invite you," Maddock said. He had positioned himself with his feet squared, his right hand dangling near the butt of the .44.

"Well," Lucky said evenly, calmly, quietly, "I don't reckon in a free country I have to wait for someone to invite me to talk."

"Dust eater, I think you're ready to leave," Maddock said, tensing.

"No," Lucky said softly, "I'm going to have one more drink, and then I'm going to leave."

"I think you're going to leave now," Maddock said, his voice rising, his odd, lifeless eyes staring.

"I think even you can see, Maddock, that I'm not packing," Lucky said, putting down his drink. "Now, if you'd care to discuss this without that hogleg—"

There were whoops of laughter. "He's got you, Craw," Wilson said, chuckling. "He doesn't have a gun. If you want to clear the air of dust in here, you'll have to do it bare-handed."

Maddock's right hand was clenching and unclenching. Men laughed.

"What's the matter, Craw?" someone yelled. "Can't you handle a desert rat bare-handed?"

"I ain't gonna break my knuckles on his hard head," Craw said, the .44 appearing in his hand as if by magic. "I reckon a little pistol-whipping will do him."

Lucky didn't move until Craw started bringing the .44 downward, aimed for the top of Lucky's head. Then he twisted aside, seized Craw's arm, and smashed his gun hand against the bar. The Colt clattered onto the bar just as Lucky's left fist flattened Craw's thin nose. Craw got in a couple of licks, one solid enough to sting Lucky's eye, then Lucky connected with a right and a left, the last a haymaker brought up from about three feet west of his belt buckle. It was over, and Craw was sliding down the bar front, his odd eyes glassy.

"Bartender," Lucky said, his voice still quiet, calm. "I'll have that last drink now."

Chunk Wilson, glowering, nodded to two men who had been watching the brief fight. A fist landed heavily on the nape of Lucky's neck, stunning him, buckling his knees. Going down, he got in a kick that almost made one of the men a gelding, and then another of Wilson's men was joining in. They lifted him and he tried to move his face away from an oncoming fist, felt the thud of it, saw a skyful of bloated, light-streaming stars, felt other thuds, and then he was moaning and trying to lift his lips out of the dust. His eyes hurt. His mouth and nose hurt. He hurt all over. He managed to crack one eye, then closed it immediately. He lifted himself on his hands and cracked open the eye again. He was on the dirt street in front of the saloon.

An eternity later he was on his feet. The wooden steps leading to the boardwalk in front of the saloon were each a mile high. The walk was two miles across, and the swinging door to the saloon weighed a ton. The place was still crowded. Lucky held himself together and walked to the bar. The bartender shook his head as he examined the wreckage of Lucky's face.

Lucky looked around, squinting around the swelling of his eyes. He saw neither Crawford nor Wilson. "How many jumped me?" he asked the bartender.

"Look, son," the bartender said, "was I you, I'd just go on about my business and get out of Socorro."

Lucky thought about it. "I'll have that last drink now," he said.

"On the house," the bartender said, pouring.

Lucky swished the raw whiskey around in his mouth, winced when it burned the cuts. He felt his teeth and they were all there, none of them loose. He grinned bloodily at the bartender. "You give good advice, friend," he said. He killed his drink and went about the business of buying beans, sugar, coffee, a small bag of flour, and a totally extravagant tin of maple syrup. He tried to forget the hurt and the ache and the cold anger that seemed to hang like lead in his gut by thinking of a breakfast of fatback and flapjacks covered with maple syrup. He slept in the stable and was on his way with the sun.

He camped once more on the bank of the Rio Grande. The cool water soothed his aches and pains. There was nothing he could do about the swelling around his eyes. He was beginning to look like a raccoon. He brewed bitter coffee by boiling it over the fire and considered the activities in Socorro. He simply did not understand unfriendly people. He thought about Maddy, then about Catalina, which brought her father to mind. He chuckled, thinking that it was a good thing that Osa hadn't been there in the saloon when men laughed at Dos Caballos.

Men were, indeed, peculiar critters. What fun did a man get out of belittling another man, of laughing at him and the place he chose to live? Not that Dos Caballos was all that much, an isolated adobe town, peopled by folks who were pretty peculiar themselves, if for nothing else for choosing to live in a place like Dos Caballos. Still, it wasn't right to laugh at a man or his chosen place to live. Maybe he should have gone to the stable and gotten the old Navy Colt—and then he might be in Socorro's boot hill by now, shot down by a man who liked killing people. Maybe there was some other way. It wasn't the beating so much. He'd lost a fight or two in his time. To his surprise he realized that he resented them laughing at Dos Caballos more than he resented them laughing at him. He'd been laughed at by experts. Maybe there was a way to have the last laugh. Chunk Wilson wore fancy, tailored suits and looked prosperous, but maybe there was a way.

Chapter Two

Lucky made camp in mid-afternoon not two miles from Dos Caballos and waited until midnight to sneak into the town. He didn't want anyone, especially Catalina, to see him looking like a swollen-eyed raccoon with a red nose and broken lips. People saw Jughead and the mule in the corral next morning, but no one saw Lucky for a few days, and no one thought much about it. Lucky, they thought, was as peculiar as anyone else in Dos Caballos. Either Lucky wanted to be alone or he'd hiked out into the mountains after deer, Osa Carranza figured, when Lucky didn't show up in the Dos Caballos Cantina.

When Lucky did decide to go to the cantina, he had to duck his head to keep from bumping it on the door. He had his shirt collar turned up, a scarf around his neck, and his hat pulled low over his eyes. He straightened his gangling frame, removed the faded, once-black hat to free unruly hair badly in need of a trim, and used the hat to billow dust from his much-washed woolen trousers.

"Why you not knock off the sheep dung outside?" asked Catalina Carranza, she of the huge, dark eyes.

Lucky put his hat back on and tugged on it. He no longer bothered to point out to Catalina that a little dust wasn't going to spoil the cantina's decor of hard dirt floor under time-darkened cedar beams that held up a brush roof covered with adobe mud. A rough cedar bench ran along one wall. Four plank tables with hard, straight-backed chairs occupied the dirt floor.

"You're burning the chili again, Osa," Lucky said, sniffing the air as he plunked a booted foot onto the rail and leaned his elbows on the polished cedar bar. The smell of the chili came from the back room where a huge, iron pot simmered perpetually on the cook stove.

"Do you eat or drink?" Osa asked, using a forearm as thick as an ordinary man's thigh to wield a filthy rag across the already burnished bar in front of Lucky. Osa looked to be past forty. He was a dark, hairy bear of a man, larger than most Mexicans.

"Beer," Lucky said.

"No credit," Osa said.

"That's your middle name," Lucky said. "No credit."

The smiling, chubby Mexican woman who peered around the door from the cantina's kitchen to see who had arrived in the middle of a sun-drugged, sweltering afternoon was not Osa's wife. As far as anyone knew, Osa never had had a wife, although he definitely had a daughter who was no more than half Mex. She had huge, dark Spanish eyes with long, thick, black lashes and that delicate and sultry coloring of skin.

Osa poured thick, foaming beer into a glass that was clean but looked as if it had been scoured in the dry dust that swirled outside. Osa made his own beer from a secret recipe he said had been brought into the Fray Cristobal Mountains by his grandfather back when the Spanish were still working the gold mines. The beer was potent. As if to prove its vigor, a bottle of the latest batch exploded its cork with a sound like a muted pistol shot. Osa picked up Lucky's dime.

"So how was your trip?" Osa asked.

"Interesting," Lucky said. He'd been doing a lot of thinking. For what he planned to do, he'd need help, mainly in the form of money. He figured that Osa had more money than anyone else in Dos Caballos. "Got lost," he said, grinning.

"Bad luck," Osa said.

Bowen Lockhart had been dozing with his feet cocked up on a table. He moaned a little, dropped his feet, and opened his eyes.

"Howdy, Bowen," Lucky said, not expecting an answer. Bowen didn't talk much. He came down regularly from his crumbling, ancient adobe hut up in the hills to enjoy the atmosphere of the cantina while he drank from a bottle of real Scotch whiskey that Osa kept especially for him.

"Not bad luck," Lucky said.

"How can it be good luck to get lost?" Osa demanded, losing his head for a moment in his curiosity and topping off Lucky's beer.

"Well, it depends on what you find, Osa," Lucky said, chugging the beer down.

Catalina the beautiful swish-swayed her long, dark skirts into the main room and went to Bowen's table. "Something, Señor Bowen?" she asked.

Lucky didn't understand Catalina's fascination with Bowen. He was the one client of the Dos Caballos who got a semblance of politeness from her, and he was as peculiar a Scot as Lucky had ever seen, although, in all honesty, he had to admit that he hadn't seen many. Bowen may have smiled at one time or the other since arriving in Dos Caballos almost a year ago, but if so, no one had seen the smile through his untrimmed beard. As for talk, a two-word greeting from Bowen was a lengthy conversation. Lucky thought that it was Bowen's silence that made him a man of mystery for Catalina. And it was obvious why Osa liked Bowen—Bowen paid for his Scotch and an occasional bowl of fiery beef and beans with hard cash.

To Lucky, Bowen was just another of the desert rats who, to the amusement of many—not Lucky, since he was often the butt of laughter himself because of his luck, he was disinclined to laugh at any other man—believed that there was still gold in the Fray Cristobals, that the Spaniard, Pedro de Abalos, who first discovered gold in 1683, and those who followed him in the two centuries since, had not ripped all of the rich, yellow metal out of the hills.

Gold had brought Osa's grandfather to the Fray Cristobals, but the only gold seen by Osa's worthy ancestor had already been panned, or mined, and crossed his counter in exchange for a bowl of chili and a beer. Since the time of the early Spanish explorers, gold—or the hope of it—had brought men into the wildness that was New Mexico. Most said that all the gold in the Fray Cristobals was gone, ripped out by the Spaniards. A few persistent desert rats like Heck Logan panned a little pay dirt from the stream higher up in the hills, but just enough to keep them in coffee and beans. The experts, the old-timers, said it was all gone, even while they traipsed the deserts and the dry hills with long, dirty white beards and a few prospecting tools carried on the back of a little donkey. When their thirst brought them to the Dos Caballos Cantina, they shook their hairy white heads and said, "It's all gone."

But was it gone, all the gold? Osa Carranza had never been able to bring himself to believe that it was. There were, after all, still working mines up around Santa Fe, and the Ortiz mine still produced good ore. Maybe, just maybe, somewhere out there, somewhere up there, the mother lode waited. Maybe, just maybe, this unlucky gringo, this Lucky, had found something. Osa knew Lucky well enough to know that he wasn't a liar. Osa wanted to believe, and when one wants to believe, believing is easy.

"Hey, you, Lucky," Osa said. "Have another beer."

"One's the limit of my daily budget," Lucky said, rising, touching his hat, turning away. He had planted the seed. He'd seen the interest flare in Osa's dark eyes. He'd bide his time now.

The sunlight cut through the pure, high air like brilliant knives. The town that had taken its name from the cantina slumbered around Lucky. The adobe huts climbed the sides of the canyon and looked down on the sparkling stream that represented the only water this side of Socorro. Lucky examined the town with a mildly querulous expression. He didn't share Osa Carranza's civic pride, maybe because his grandfather and father hadn't lived in Dos Caballos. Lucky couldn't quite understand why Osa's grandfather had built a cantina in such a desolate location in the first place, at least not until he'd made sure that the Overland Mail route was going to make Dos Caballos a way station, and thus a center of trade. The stage route had bypassed Dos Caballos, in spite of the fact that the route through the town would have cut off a hundred miles east to west. Lucky supposed it was the roads that had made the stage company decide to bypass Dos Caballos to the south. They were old Spanish roads, the newest of them built in 1833 to carry supplies to and gold from the working mines. They were narrow, rough, mountainous, and subject to rock slides.

But, as Osa was fond of saying, Dos Caballos could never be called a one-horse town. Time and events might pass it by, but it would always have its name, a grand-sounding name that rolled well on the tongue in

Spanish but lost something when Dos Caballos was translated into Two Horses.

Lucky walked up the street, his boots making little puffs of dust. He was still savoring the memory of Catalina Carranza, telling himself that the girl was young, just eighteen, and that there might be hope for him yet, hope even for a man whose luck often ran against him.

Lucky Smith had had enough luck, all bad, to last most men two lifetimes, or to see them sleeping peacefully in the lonesome Dos Caballos cemetery. Perhaps it was idle dreaming on his part to wonder how it would feel to run his fingers through that flowing mass of ebony hair and to get a smile from Catalina instead of that patrician stare down her lovely, long nose.

When he reached his own establishment, Lucky stopped, leaned against a weathered wall, put one boot heel up, and once again surveyed Dos Caballos. There were times when Lucky felt like following the example of the former owner of the stable, who had decided that he had had about all of the Dos Caballos type of prosperity he could stand and simply had walked away. Thinking about that, Lucky had some hope. Taking over the stable had been a bit of luck, not bad. And a man whose luck was always bad couldn't complain about being stuck away in a two-horse town in the dry mountains just south of the Jordana del Muerto, a full fifty miles from the nearest point of civilization in Socorro.

Osa Carranza wiped his polished bar and kept a baleful eye on his daughter, who was humming and dancing to her own music. He looked suspiciously at Bowen Lockhart, but Bowen had gone back to sleep. If Catalina, whose natural charm and overt friendliness often gave a newcomer to the cantina the wrong idea, was indeed dancing for Bowen's eyes, she was earning little reward. That made it good for Bowen Lockhart, because Osa would kill rather than see Catalina marry some desert rat.

Osa was always on a thin edge regarding his daughter. Her gregarious personality and her natural beauty were, of course, good for business, and her father was, after all, a saloon keeper, a kindhearted man who bled inside each time he had to use his thick cedar club on the skull of an amorous cowboy or sheepherder who'd been misled by Catalina's sparkling black eyes.

Osa worried more about Bowen Lockhart than about most men simply because Bowen never talked enough to give a man an inkling of his intentions. He didn't worry at all about Lucky Smith, because it was obvious that Catalina had too much good common sense to consider an alliance with a man whose luck was always bad. In fact, Osa rather liked Lucky. He was an easygoing, lanky, slow-talking man who didn't go around burdening people with his tales of woe. You'd never hear from Lucky how he came to the Fray Cristobals with a small herd of sheep, a young wife, a small son, and high hopes. No, Lucky never mentioned his past. It was left to others to talk about how, in an effort to improve the grazing on the parcel of land he'd occupied, he'd set fire to the sparse grass only to see the desert brush burst into a wildfire that consumed the shack he'd built for his family, with his family inside. His luck held when, after reading an English book about sheep husbandry, he followed directions exactly to mix a dip that was supposed to rid his sheep of ticks and fleas and then stood helplessly by as all of his animals died in agony.

There'd been some behind-the-hand chuckling and giggling when, since no one else wanted it, Lucky moved into the abandoned stable and blacksmith shop. Money exchanged hands in bets on the exact date when disaster would strike in the form of fire, lightning, or storm. Lucky began to replace dry-rotted planks, taught himself how to fashion horseshoes—that was about the only cash business he could expect—and aside from being kicked in the head a couple of times by mules who didn't take kindly to his shoeing touch, he had survived to become a part of Dos Caballos.

Lucky was well liked in town. After a while people stopped laughing at him, even when they saw straw in his hair when he removed his once-black hat to dust off his breeches. Not that anyone had ever laughed much to Lucky's face. He didn't become belligerent, didn't object, but a certain look came into his steel-gray eyes, a look that made men wonder if there wasn't some hidden strength there that was directly at odds with Lucky's mild manner and sun-bleached looks.

The afternoon advanced, and Catalina had left the cantina to rest moodily in the living quarters. Osa leaned on the bar and dozed. Bowen Lockhart, after another drink, slept soundly in his chair, his mouth a cavity in the wildness of his beard, from which issued snorts and growlings. Lucky, thinking of the coach, was sitting on the bench in front of the stables. Zelma Clemmons, a stolid, big, red-faced woman, came slowly up the street and sat beside Lucky on the bench.

"I hear you've been down the hill," Zelma said.

"Yeah," Lucky admitted.

"Long trip when you can buy what you need here," Zelma said.

"Well," Lucky said.

"Our prices ain't too high when you consider that we have to haul the stuff all the way up here."

"Well, it isn't the price," Lucky said, although it was very definitely the price that sent him off now and then on a fifty-mile pack. He didn't, however, want to hurt Zelma's feelings by telling her so.

Zelma looked up at the blazing sun and sighed. "Looks like them folks back East gonna have their war."

"Oh?" Lucky asked. "That's what the newspapers say?"

"Got a newspaper no more'n a month old," Zelma said. "Don't really recollect who done started it, didn't read it all, but they's fightin' in some place called Fort Sumter, down in South Carolina."

"Too bad," Lucky said. The news was of events that were happening in another world.

"Old man Butterworth done sold the Overland Mail," Zelma said.

"Sold it, huh?"

"Lock, stock, and barrel. New owner says he's gonna abandon the southern routes and go straight to Californee through Salt Lake City."

"Well," Lucky said. He sat up straight. Zelma's month-old newspaper had made what he'd heard in Socorro official. He wondered if Osa had heard the news. With stage service discontinued in the Southwest, Dos Caballos would become even more isolated. He figured that the time was about right to approach Osa with a business proposition.

Chapter Three

Osa Carranza had been thinking about what Lucky had said for twenty-four hours when Lucky ducked his way into the Dos Caballos Cantina again.

"Hey, Lucky, I feel generous today. Have one on me," Osa said, coming halfway around the bar.

"Well, Osa, if you insist," Lucky said, grinning happily as Osa poured.

"You got lost," Osa said. "Tell me."

"Well, you know," Lucky said, "I was going along sort of addle-pated and thinking deep thoughts . . ."

"You were asleep in the saddle," Osa translated, "letting the horse keep the trail."

"And there I was on one of those old Spanish roads," Lucky said.

The old Spanish roads had been built for two reasons: to get to the mines and to get gold out. Osa's eyes gleamed.

"You found something. You said it was interesting," Osa said as he topped off Lucky's beer again.

"You're going to get me pie-eyed, Osa," Lucky said.

"Interesting."

"Well, yes, it was, sorta," Lucky said.

"Lucky, you remember that Osa Carranza had always been you friend." Osa spoke American better than most of the locals, but when he was excited he sometimes slipped.

"*Tu amigo,* Lucky," Osa said.

"Osa, you would never sell me a beer on credit, not even when I had a job lined up and had money coming."

"Hey, Lucky, I don't sell nobody nothing on credit," Osa said, hands outspread.

"Well, Osa, I guess we are friends, aren't we?" Lucky asked, finishing his beer.

"Sure, sure," Osa said. "Look, you need anything—anything for this thing you have found, this interesting thing?"

"As a matter of fact, Osa," Lucky said, "it would be helpful if you'd lend me your wagon for a few days."

"No credit, no lending," Osa said automatically, then he cringed and asked, "For why you need the wagon?"

"Oh, well," Lucky said, turning away, "I just thought it would be friendly of you to lend it to me."

"Why you need the wagon?" Osa said, his Mex accent getting the better of him in his frustration. "Why you ask me to lend you my wagon without telling me why? You want to borrow my wagon and you don't tell Osa nothing, or give him a chance to get in on . . ." He paused, wondering why Lucky was grinning. He noticed that there were dark spots of old lividity around Lucky's eyes. Lucky's grin made him want to pick up his cedar club and give Lucky another bruise right on top of his head.

Lucky leaned on the bar. "Well, Osa, I didn't think you'd be interested in buying into a certain enterprise, so I didn't mention it. I just thought maybe you'd lend me the wagon for a couple days, maybe three."

"Is good?" Osa said, visions of the mother lode in his dark eyes.

"Pretty good," Lucky said. "I think it has promise."

"Look," Osa said, "take the wagon. Take it for as long as you need." His face became agonized as he pictured what this gringo's luck could possibly do to his wagon. "Just be careful, huh?" He smiled. "And when you know more, we talk, eh? We talk partners, all right, amigo?"

20

"Sure, Osa. I was thinking I might need a partner. It was just that I thought you wouldn't be interested."

"Take the wagon," Osa said expansively. "You need anything else?"

Lucky had one job to do. The Widow Brown, owner and operator of the boardinghouse, had been after him for weeks to fix the damper in the sitting-room fireplace. He, being a man of conscience, took a faceful of chimney soot while removing the damper, coughed, spat, and said, "Dadgum" with such intensity that the Widow Brown blushed, making her fat, red face even redder. He had to fashion a new pin for the damper mechanism, and that killed the day. So he didn't hitch a very insulted and indignant Jughead in harness with old Coaly in front of Osa's wagon until just after dawn the next morning. Osa came pouring out of the living quarters behind the cantina in his nightshirt, a long, mean-looking antique musket in his hand, only to jerk to a halt and look in wonderment at Lucky's unlikely team.

"Morning, Osa," Lucky said. "Didn't mean to wake you."

Osa, speechless, leaned on the musket and watched the wagon rattle away, Jughead looking back reproachfully at Lucky, his brown eyes sparkling his indignity.

Even before the job was begun, Lucky was questioning his own sanity. It took him a couple of days to hack and cut his way from the lower road into the canyon, and another half day to clear a turnaround near the wrecked Concord coach. Then and only then did he reexamine the smashed, rusted, broken, discolored hodgepodge of a mess of a wrecked stagecoach. It would, he felt, take a genius to put that wreckage back together, and once it was done, what would he have? He'd need at least four, preferably six, good horses to pull the coach, and then he'd have no place to go.

He sat down on a nearby rock and thought about it for a while, flicking sweat from his forehead. Heck, if nothing else, he could hook up old Jughead and Coaly to the coach and take Catalina for a ride. That pleasant prospect did for him what his fading resolution to have the last laugh on Chunk Wilson and his men could not, and he set about loading pieces onto the wagon. He hauled the first load into Dos Caballos under cover of darkness, slept in the loft on his bed of straw, and was back in the canyon by noon for another load. He'd lost his chance to forget the whole affair, for once he started something, he was inclined to finish it.

He took the partitions down between two unused stalls in the stable, kept the doors barred from the inside. People didn't ordinarily visit unless invited, but the stable was, after all, a place of public business. He didn't want someone coming in wanting a horse shoed to see the wreckage before he had a chance to work on it. Once he had the whole mess in the stable, in a scattered arrangement with all parts roughly in relative positions to each other, he didn't know whether to say "Dadgum" or "Woo-ha." It was late by the time he'd returned Osa's wagon and avoided his curious questions. He examined the wreckage by lantern light and began to admire the workmanship of those craftsmen who had fashioned the coach way back East in New Hampshire. Somewhere, he'd heard it said that the Concord coach got its durability from the use of a high mountain oak—strong, durable—and he believed it. He wouldn't have any wood like that, but he could come up with bois d'arc, called bo-dark in the West, and dry, iron-hard cedar. He'd have to maybe special-order some fancy paint through the general store in Socorro.

In his first act of restoration, Lucky polished a piece of brass. Then he was hooked, because the brass had weathered its years in the sun well and now gleamed like gold. In his sleep, Lucky dreamed of the splendor of a pristine Concord: gleaming yellow and red, brass shining, bouncing along on the thoroughbraces made of eight layers of heavy leather running fore and aft from between the iron stanchions attached to the undercarriage. The leather thoroughbraces would do a better job of cushioning bumps than any set of springs known to man and could be replaced regularly. He dreamed of the coach leaving Dos Caballos with two sets of three passengers facing each other on the leather seats inside, three more perched on the backless seats in the middle, and three men on the seat behind the driver, himself, atop. Out front were six glowing white horses of unsurpassed beauty. Then he woke to see the same mess piled in the stalls.

After breakfast he set to straightening the bent rims of the smashed wheels. Straight rims were no use without spokes and wheels, so the next step was to go wandering off with his ax and Jughead and old Coaly to find bois d'arc for the spokes, and cedar for the rims. Once Osa tried to follow him, sneaking in and out of the brush and trees like a bandit, so Lucky waited and asked him if he'd care to give him a hand. When Osa saw that Lucky was out after wood, he rolled his eyes and made himself scarce with a mumbled excuse that Catalina was alone at the Dos Caballos Cantina. Osa spent the rest of the day trying to figure out why Lucky needed wood and decided with a flash of genius that Lucky must be building his own wagon, in order to cut Osa out of the mother lode. In a fit of dark anger, Osa resolved never to speak to Lucky again and to use the cedar club the next time Lucky came in to get a dime for the beer Lucky had tricked him into giving away for free.

Lucky made another trip down the hill and, to his surprise, found that the paints and materials he needed were in stock at the general store in Socorro. He was back home as quickly as possible, not having bothered to wash the dust from his throat in a Socorro saloon, and he was, without knowing it, the talk of Dos Caballos.

"What's he doing up there?" Mack Clemmons asked on one of his trips back to the general store, once again without even a trace of gold dust.

"Osa thinks he's building a wagon," Zelma said.

"Why does he keep the outer doors closed on a hot day like this?" Mack wanted to know.

"He ain't making horseshoes," Osa grumbled to a silent Bowen Lockhart as they sat in the cool of the evening on the cantina's front porch.

Lucky's hammer was ringing. Smoke from his forge coiled darkly upward into the brilliant evening sky.

Catalina, leaning on the back of Bowen's chair, asked, "Why you don't go see, if it bothers you?"

"Why don't you—" Osa said, correcting Catalina's speech.

"Because I don't give a damn," Catalina said.

Osa was too angry with Lucky to explain to Catalina that he hadn't been asking her to go. He poured Bowen another glass, having brought the diminishing bottle of Scotch onto the porch, and gazed off into the west, where the sun was painting the horizon in fiery glory.

For her part, Catalina was curious too. It wasn't like Lucky to stay away from the Dos Caballos Cantina for days, weeks. It wasn't that she missed him—*caramba*, no. She had no more intention of wasting herself on a desert rat—and all residents of Dos Caballos and the surrounding wilderness fell into that category—than her father had of allowing her to do so. Only the previous night she had asked her father, once more, "When will you take me to San Francisco?"

"It is not yet time," Osa had said. "You are not yet old enough."

"I am eighteen," she'd argued. "Soon I will be the old maid."

"I will tell you when," Osa had said, mentally counting his store of gold and silver coins, buried so carefully under loose floorboards in his bedroom.

So Catalina, maybe as much out of curiosity as to why Lucky hadn't been in the cantina making calf eyes at her as out of wanting to know what he was doing, often late into the night, undulated her way up the street just after dark and climbed the outside ladder into the loft of the stable where Lucky kept his digs. She stumbled over a chair and almost knocked it over before her eyes adjusted to the greater darkness inside. By the glow of reflected light from a full moon, she examined Lucky's home: a little iron stove, a cot with straw sticking out from under a blanket, the chair, and a couple of changes of clothing hanging on nails on the plank wall.

She went out of the little room into the hayloft and paused to hear a handsaw making slow, rasping cuts, and then the tapping of Lucky's hammer. She crawled on her hands and knees to look down into the stable, and her dark, large eyes went wide. Lucky was just putting the finishing touches on the coach, and he had it gleaming in splendor, brass golden and reflecting the light of two or three lanterns, wood freshly painted, iron parts free of rust and painted yellow. Catalina was so enrapt by the sight of the gleaming, polished coach that she didn't notice for a moment that Lucky had stripped to the waist. Her eyes widened even more. In his baggy clothing, Lucky didn't look like much. Bare to the waist, his arms were long but strong, well muscled without being brawny. His back and chest were bare of any hint of fat, with muscles that, wet with his sweat, gleamed and writhed as he worked. In spite of herself, she gasped and then cried out as, swift as any striking snake, Lucky had dropped the hammer and was pointing his Navy Colt at her startled face, peering down over the edge of the hayloft.

"Dadgum, Catalina, you scared me out of a year's growth," Lucky said, lowering the gun. Then his own eyes went wide. "What are you doing here?"

"What are you doing here?" Catalina countered, regaining her dignity and standing.

Lucky swallowed as trim ankles were revealed, along with a hint of calf encased in white hose, as Catalina climbed down the ladder.

"This is what?" Catalina asked.

"Nice of you to come visiting," Lucky said.

"This is a stagecoach?"

"Uh, yeah," Lucky said, sinking deeply into those dark, Spanish eyes.

"What for is the stagecoach?"

"Well, I thought I'd take you for a ride," Lucky said.

"Hmmph," Catalina said, walking around to the other side of the coach to study the pretty scrollwork.

"I'm sure glad you came," Lucky said, thinking that at last his luck was changing even as he cast a look skyward and Godward and thus toward Maddy to ask forgiveness for what he'd started thinking after seeing Catalina's ankles.

"I didn't come to see you," she said, giving him the down-her-nose look.

"Whatever . . . I'm glad," he said. "Can I offer you a cup of coffee?"

"I will go now," Catalina said. She went to the main doors and started trying to lift the heavy bar.

"You don't have to go," Lucky said, coming to her side.

"Oh, yes, I do," she said. "Let me out or I will scream."

"Dadgum," Lucky said. "I didn't let you in."

"You will let me out, though."

"Sure." He opened the small, man-size door beside the big doors and watched in puzzlement as she swayed down the street. He heard the peal of her laughter as she reached the porch of the cantina, where Osa and Bowen still sat, and then the deeper sound of male laughter. He closed the door and stood there for a while with his head down, and then he went back to the coach.

Chapter Four

Not that it mattered anymore, since the whole town knew and was laughing at Lucky's Folly. He kept the door closed during the couple of days following Catalina's visit that it took him to put the last, delicate finishing touches on his masterwork. He didn't care who laughed; it was, dadgum it, a beauty, that coach. He spent just about the whole day admiring it, climbing into the driver's seat to imagine the wind of motion in his face, six white horses out front, sitting inside to measure the comfort of the passengers on the new cowhide seat covers. He wished for the skill of some of the Mex artisans who worked in silver so that he could stud it up a bit and pretty it up with silverwork, but since he had no silver, he'd have to settle for what he had. Which, he decided, wasn't bad.

It was one hell of a beautiful day. Lucky didn't notice it but others did, and for some reason, almost as if the messages were going out mentally or something, it became one of those gathering days in Dos Caballos when the desert rats and sheepherders and prospectors and panners all came to town at just about the same time, making it a profitable, as well as a beautiful, day for Osa.

When Lucky decided that he'd had enough looking at his work, he took a quick bath in the inside horse trough and put on a clean change of clothes and ambled out into the dying day whistling. It was time to celebrate. He'd go as high as three beers at the Dos Caballos Cantina and let them laugh as they might, because he'd unveil the coach the next morning and then see how they laughed.

Probably no more than one or two of the residents and occasional visitors to Dos Caballos knew the date, May 24, 1861. None of them knew that back East, North Carolina, the eleventh and last southern state, had seceded from the Union. Ben Butler's Confederate Army had moved out of Fort Monroe toward Hampton, Virginia, the day before. And on that very day, although the news of it wouldn't reach Dos Caballos until someone went down and brought back a newspaper, federal troops crossed the Potomac at Washington and occupied Alexandria. All that would not have interested Lucky too much if he'd known. He had finished his coach and was going to have his first beer in weeks.

"Hey, Lucky," Luke Malloy yelled when Lucky ducked into the cantina. Luke was a sheepherder who didn't mind at all when people said he was, without doubt, the shaggiest, dirtiest, most ragged sheepherder in New Mexico. "We thought you'd be in Californee in that fancy stagecoach of yourn."

"Need six mules like you to pull it, Luke," Lucky yelled back.

The Dos Caballos had attracted a very large crowd, a full twelve patrons, including two Mexican women and Zelma Clemmons. Osa was behind the bar pouring beer and beaming, and Catalina shot Lucky a very unusual smile as she flitted toward a table with a tray holding bowls of steaming chili.

"What you gonna do with that stagecoach?" Mack Clemmons asked as Lucky walked past, headed toward the bar.

"Well, Mack"—Lucky grinned—"I might just sleep in it, since it is prettier inside than any house this side of San Francisco."

"A stagecoach," Osa said. "A *perniciosa* stagecoach. No credit."

"No credit," Lucky said, tossing coins onto the bar. *"Es muy guapa."*

"A stagecoach," Osa said, pouring. He was having great difficulty giving up the dream of sharing a mother lode with Lucky.

"I'm celebrating tonight," Lucky said after a sip. "We'll talk tomorrow, Osa."

"We have nothing to talk," Osa said. "Except you owe me a dime for that beer I gave you."

Lucky raised an eyebrow. Osa growled and went to pour for another customer. He was going to have to break into a green batch of his home brew if business kept up into the evening, and by that time he wanted everyone to be past caring.

Mack and Zelma Clemmons were engaged in a family dispute, with Zelma's voice going shrill. Catalina was singing happily, having so many men with whom to flirt. Luke Malloy was telling how he'd almost been eaten by a "painter" out in them godforsaken mountains. Everyone else was conducting the serious business of socializing at the top of their voices. The sudden silence that fell caused Osa to reach for his club and Lucky to turn around from the bar. In the door, his head just clearing the lintel, was a startling vision, a thick-chested, clean-shaven, hair-brushed-and-trimmed man in—

"Dadgum," Lucky said.

—a skirt.

Osa froze, the cedar club half raised. Catalina's mouth was open, showing an enticing pink tongue and gleaming, white teeth. Even Zelma Clemmons, who'd been telling Mack once and for all that his days of traipsing the hills were over, was silent. Luck Malloy had his beer mug almost to his lips, tilted, so that yeasty foam was dripping over the rim to make mud pies on his ragged woolen trousers.

The vision walked, erect and proud, to the bar. "My bottle, Osa," it said.

Osa was paralyzed, club still half-raised. "Huh?"

"The whiskey," the vision in skirt said, and Osa recognized the voice.

"Bowen?" Osa asked, lowering the club.

Lucky, a few feet away, was entranced by the man's splendor. The dark, somber tartan ended at the man's knobby knees. The lower legs were encased in hose. A gleam of very clean linen showed at Bowen's throat, with ruffles, and, quite impressive, a red plume extended from his headdress.

"That you, Bowen?" Lucky asked.

Bowen Lockhart, in the full parade dress of the Black Watch regiment, took his private bottle of Scotch whiskey from Osa's trembling hand, poured into a not-too-clean glass, turned, and said, "Ye will all stand."

To a man—and a woman—they obeyed.

"Ye will lift yer glasses in a toast to the Queen, for 'tis her own birthday," Bowen said.

"What queen is that?" Mack Clemmons asked.

"Does it matter?" Zelma asked. "Since when have you needed an excuse to drink?"

Glasses were lifted.

"To the Queen," Bowen said, his voice surprisingly full and loud. "Victoria, Queen of the United Kingdom of Great Britain and Ireland, Empress of India."

"Suits me," Mack Clemmons said, drinking.

Glasses tilted.

"You will now repeat after me," Bowen said, "three times together, 'Long live the Queen.' "

"Don't we get to drink again?" Mack asked.

"How 'bout singing 'Happy Birthday'?" Catalina asked, trying to get the attention of the most beautiful man—damn the skirt—she'd ever seen. If she had known Bowen Lockhart looked like that cleaned up, she'd have thrown him in the horse trough long ago.

"Long live the Queen," Bowen began, and the ceremony ran its course with only one giggle from Luke Malloy, quickly silenced by a glare from Bowen's hard blue eyes.

"What do he wear under that thing?" Luke whispered.

"I have only one more word fer ye," Bowen said, "for I cannot help but note your curiosity. What I wear is the tartan of the Black Watch, King George's own, and that's all ye need to know."

Bowen turned to the bar. Gradually the talk resumed, on a reduced noise level. Shaggy Luke Malloy edged up beside Lucky at the bar. "I hearn of them kilts," he whispered. "Always puzzled me no end what them Scot fellers wore under 'em."

"I don't think I'd ask, Luke," Lucky said.

Luke fumbled for a dime and got a fresh beer, drank it, his sun-browned, soiled face screwed into questioning torment above his greasy beard. Mack and Zelma Clemmons went back to their perennial discussion of Mack's frequent absences.

"I jest gotta know," Luke Malloy said, weaving around Lucky to stand beside Bowen. Lucky moved back a few feet. Luke leaned close but Lucky didn't catch the words. A scowl darkened Bowen's face.

"That is not a proper question to ask," he said.

Luke seemed to accept that. He turned, staggering only a little, and took one step before whirling to grab for Bowen's kilt.

For the first time Dos Caballos saw Bowen Lockhart smile. It was a grim smile that widened into sheer pleasure as his fist found Luke's nose. Luke, not a small man under all his shagginess, landed a good one in Bowen's gut. Bowen whooped with joy, and for a couple of minutes it was touch-and-go as, surprisingly, Luke held his own. Bowen was smiling all the while, and the smile became even wider when Mack Clemmons, totally unable to withhold himself from the fun any longer, launched himself at the battling pair with the intention of lifting Bowen's kilt to satisfy the curiosity of all.

No one enjoyed a good fight more than Osa. He wasn't concerned when two other men took sides, one with Bowen and one with Mack and Luke, and a chair smashed under a falling body. It had been a long time since the cantina had seen such a spirited fracas, and Osa was sore put to stay out of it, but it was necessary for him to stay behind the bar to protect, with his cedar club, the only thing of value in the cantina, the bottles on the shelves, his stock-in-trade.

Lucky saw that more of the men were siding with the curious than with Bowen. He finished his beer; sighed; moved forward with deceptive, lanky awkwardness; and sent Mack Clemmons flying into a table with a well-placed left to the cheek. The table splintered, and Mack rolled over, looking as if he were asleep. Someone caught Lucky's eye with a fist, and then for a while it was just a blur of motion until he found himself standing back to back with Bowen at the bar, only the two Mexican women and Zelma Clemmons conscious, all three seated on the cedar bench along the wall.

"Gentlemen," Bowen said, bowing to first Osa and then to Lucky, "I thank you for joining me in a most enjoyable Queen's Birthday celebration."

Chapter Five

Osa was on the back porch of the living quarters, splashing cold water onto his face. The sun was just peeking over the eastern hills. He was bare to the waist, showing a little roll of fat above his tight trousers.

"I don't lend my wagon," he said as Lucky slinked around the corner of the cantina and leaned against a porch post.

"I figured you'd be in a good mood after all the fun last night," Lucky said.

"Good fight," Osa said, grinning to show a fine set of teeth under his mustache. "Your eye is black again."

"Yeah, dadgum it, same place as before," Lucky said.

"No credit, no lending," Osa said, recovering from his moment of friendliness.

"I wanna talk to you, Osa."

"It's time for my breakfast."

"That's all right. I'll talk while you eat."

Osa didn't object, so Lucky followed him into the kitchen. The fat señora who cooked and cleaned served Osa a slab of bacon and a half dozen eggs with a chunk of flat Mex bread. Osa grudgingly allowed the señora to pour Lucky a cup of coffee.

"I'm thinking of running regular stage service between Dos Caballos and Socorro," Lucky said.

"Hmmph," Osa said through a mouthful.

"You think about it, Osa. You're the one always saying Dos Caballos is going to be something someday. How can the town grow when the only way you can get to it is by taking a fifty-mile horseback ride? How can we expect to pull people in to trade when everything has to be packed on muleback with prices charged accordingly?"

Osa's interest was aroused. "You'd need two or three change stations between here and Socorro. Not enough business to make that expense."

"Well, I've been thinking about that. Reason why they have change stations every ten or fifteen miles on a regular run is the need for speed, to move passengers and mail over some pretty long distances as quickly as possible. I figure anyone going to Socorro from here won't be in that much of a hurry. We walk the horses, rest them if need be. We'd need just one team that way. People up here could ride down in comfort to buy supplies, carry them back on the stage. Mack and Zelma Clemmons would be forced to come down on their prices at the general store, and everyone would benefit, even Mack and Zelma, because lower prices would bring in more people from the ranches and digs. Those living closer would come here instead of going into Socorro."

Osa wasn't ready to admit that he was interested. He just grunted.

"With stage service there just might be visitors. We got real healthy air up here, Osa. There's good hunting in the hills and trout in the stream. Visitors would be customers for the only cantina in town."

Osa's eyes squinted and took on a little gleam.

"And then there's the mail," Lucky said. "Not that anybody gets much mail up here, but it's a hit-and-miss proposition, coming up only when someone goes down to Socorro. We could make mail service regular, say once a month, or maybe even once every two weeks."

"You keep saying 'we,' " Osa said.

"I got the stage," Lucky said. "What I don't have is horses."

"Ah," Osa said. He was adding up the cost of six decent horses, and he didn't like the final figure. He figured that Lucky didn't have enough cash to buy a bridle, much less six horses and the material to make the harness for a stage team. He was doubtful about the potential profitability of the venture, and it hurt to think of taking good silver and gold from his hoard under the bedroom floorboards to throw down a dry hole. That nest egg he was accumulating was for a specific purpose. One day he was going to take Catalina off to San Francisco and marry her off to a proper gentleman, preferably from a good, honorable Spanish family.

"No," Osa said.

"Well, I'm not going to take that as your final word," Lucky said.

"Take it," Osa said. "Believe it."

"I gonna roll the coach out and let folks see it today," Lucky said.

"So?"

"I won't charge to look at it," Lucky said with a grin, then rose, having finished his coffee and seeing no inclination on Osa's part for the offer of more.

Osa went into the cantina, cleaned the bar, checked the glasses, kept looking out the window at the dusty street. He saw a few people walk by toward the stable, and he couldn't get the picture of new clients for the cantina out of his mind. He muttered a few acrid curses in Spanish and went out the front door.

Lucky had the help of Mack Clemmons and Heck Logan to roll the coach out of the stable. Women gasped in admiration as the sun caught the brass and lit the bright yellow and barn-red paint. The ornate scrollwork of the lower panels gleamed with new paint, slopped over from the original design in only a few places.

"I salvaged as much of the original wood as I could," Lucky told the small gathering. "Most of the body is made of mountain oak that grows back East. They used it because it won't shrivel up in dry conditions, like here, and won't swell when it rains."

He pointed out the genius of the coach's construction, how it was made without springs to give a better ride than sprung vehicles, how sturdy the running gear was, the way the wheel hubs were fitted to the iron axles. He kept watching for Osa and hid a grin when he saw the bearlike form coming up the street. Then he saw Catalina coming behind Osa and couldn't hide his grin anymore. He went over the whole thing again for Osa and Catalina. People began to drift away. Two small Mexican boys had coaxed Lucky to let them climb into the driver's box, and they were cracking imaginary whips and yelling out in Spanish to imaginary horses.

"It is beautiful," Catalina said. She'd been looking at Lucky with new eyes ever since she had seen him bare to the waist in the stable.

"I've reserved you the best seat for the first trip," Lucky said.

"What are you going to pull it with?" Osa asked with a sneer. "One old horse and a mule?"

"Six horses, Osa," Lucky said. "Up until a little while ago they'd have cost a hundred dollars each. Now that the Overland Mail isn't coming through anymore, we can get good stage horses for fifty each."

"Three hundred dollars," Osa said with a painful moan.

"I didn't tell you, Osa, since you didn't seem to be interested, that I wrote to the United States Post Office in Washington City asking for a mail contract to carry U.S. mail between Dos Caballos and Socorro."

Osa mumbled under his breath.

"I figure five hundred dollars will do it, Osa," Lucky said.

Osa's face showed inner agony.

"Three for the horses, the rest for harness, feed, incidentals like axle grease . . ."

Osa had tried twice to speak. The words came in a forced croak. "Seventy-five twenty-five, since I am putting up the money."

"Fifty-fifty," Lucky said, "since I have the coach and will do the work."

"Sixty-forty," Osa said, drawing himself up to his full height and sucking in his stomach.

"Equal partners or nothing," Lucky said. "I can always sleep in it."

"It will be called the Carranza Stage Company," Osa said.

"It will be called the Dos Caballos Stage Company," Lucky said. "In honor of your grandfather, who first named the cantina and the town."

"You are a gringo bandit," Osa said.

Lucky extended his hand. Slowly, after two false efforts to extend his own hand, Osa took it.

There were few timepieces and only one calendar in Dos Caballos, the calendar having been sent to the Widow Brown by her sister in St. Louis. The seasonal change to summer was the only way that Lucky marked time as he prepared to enter the business of operating the Dos Caballos Stage Company. He carried Osa's good silver and gold down the hill in Jughead's saddlebags, only to discover that Chunk Wilson had bought up all the trained stage horses. So he settled for six not-too-handsome bays from a ranch twenty miles north of Socorro. He had to fashion the reins and harness himself from materials purchased at the general store in Socorro. While he was traveling around in the world outside Dos Caballos, he heard talk of the war. John R. Raylor and his "buffalo-hunter" Confederates had proclaimed New Mexico to be southern territory, but most New Mexicans were as unconcerned as Lucky, himself, although a few bristled at what they called an invasion from Texas.

Among the more pleasant aspects about being a businessman was Catalina's new respect. Now she insisted that Lucky take a seat at a table instead of standing at the bar, and she served him with a smile that made all the hard work of cutting through the brush to get the coach out, all the hacking and cutting and carrying, all the metalwork and hammering and polishing and sanding and painting, worthwhile.

When word got around that Lucky was coming back up the hill with horses, the mountains and deserts for miles around emptied themselves of desert rats and sheepherders and a few cowboys, some of whom swallowed their disappointment when they discovered that Lucky had to fashion the riggings and harness to fit to the doubletrees on the coach's long tongue before the big event could take place. Some few of them stayed in town, much to Osa's pleasure.

When the great day dawned, a sizable crowd was on hand. There were more than enough volunteers to help Lucky roll the coach out of the stable and to position and harness the six patient bays.

To drive an overland stage the driver had to handle six sets of reins, three held in the right hand, three in the left. Lucky had watched one of Chunk Wilson's stages come wheeling into Socorro in a cloud of dust to be jerked to a halt expertly from a dead run. It looked simple enough. The driver had to be aware of which set of reins he was dealing with, and to make a short turn he had to shorten the reins of the lead horses first, then the swing horses, and finally the wheelers. Lucky had purchased himself a long whip like those used by real stage drivers, and a few hours of practice with it out behind the stable had made him, he felt, reasonably competent. The idea was not to hit the horses but to snap the whip as close to their ears as possible. Lucky knew that he'd be a little reluctant to use the whip for a while, lest he take off an ear and cause a runaway, but then he wasn't going to be trying to set any speed records.

He'd given great attention to the brakes. The way the stage horses were harnessed, they couldn't hold back a coach going downhill. That was up to the driver. He used his right foot to press on a long lever that pinched the brake shoes against the rear wheels. There'd be many steep grades on the way to the Rio Grande, so Lucky had made the brake shoes extra sturdy and extra thick.

He climbed into the driver's seat. Catalina said she wanted to be on the first ride, but Lucky told her that first he'd rather give it a try himself. She pouted but said nothing else under the stern gaze of her father, who agreed with Lucky that if anyone was going to get killed, it wasn't going to be his daughter.

Lucky looked around. He would have preferred to run the test without an audience, but there was no help for it, and he figured it was good for future business to have everyone so interested. He clucked the way he did to get old Coaly going, and the horses—it looked as if the lead horses were a mile out front—didn't even look around to see what was happening. He slapped the reins, trying to move all six at once, and managed to slap the lead horses on the rumps. They turned their heads and snorted at him.

"Hyah," Lucky yelled, getting a little anxious. He yelled again and sent the whip shooting out three feet above the ears of the lead horses and, with that "Hyah" and the snap of the whip, six horses tried to go in six different directions. The leaders bolted, jerking the harness tight, then ripped it away as the swing horses tried to back up. They ran into each other at the same time the wheelers started out in independent east and west directions. The leaders, trailing broken harness, ran a hundred yards down the street and halted to look around. One of them whinnied at Lucky as if snickering.

Osa was muttering dire Spanish curses. Catalina was hiding a giggle behind her hand. The rest of the population had one more good laugh on old Lucky. Lucky, his gray eyes narrowed and looking straight ahead, went down the street to retrieve the lead horses.

"Woo-ha," a cowboy yelled, slapping his leg with his hat. "Ain't seen nothing like that since lightning hit the outhouse."

"Look at that," someone yelled. "Old Lucky's already halfway down the hill."

"My money!" Osa groaned. "I have spent my money on a stagecoach. A stagecoach! I have spent my money on something as useless as tits on a boar."

Old Heck Logan helped Lucky push the coach back into the stable. He had done his share of laughing, but he felt like things had been just a little unfair. "By gum, Lucky," he said, "don't you feel bad. The coach moved about five feet 'fore the lead hosses broke loose."

"Well, Heck," Lucky said, "the Dos Caballos Stage Company is going to have a short run, just fifty miles, so I reckon a short beginning is in order."

But it bothered him. Hell, yes, it bothered him—to be all dressed up in clean clothes and have six fine horses out in front of a gleaming coach and his girl looking up at him with a proud smile and then to have everything go haywire. He didn't go to the cantina that night. He spent that evening and the next day repairing the damage. No one came around, and that suited him fine. He was getting just a little tired of being laughed at.

Chapter Six

Luckily a double tree and some harness had broken before the horses had ripped the tongue out of the coach. Lucky checked everything. It was late in the evening, but he had no eye for the usual glory of a sunset. He checked and rechecked; had a talk with each of the horses individually, even if they didn't understand his dire threats of making them into horsehair sofa covers if they didn't cooperate. He positioned the stage outside, well after dark, after the lights had gone out in all the houses and only Bowen Lockhart's horse was hitched up at the Dos Caballos.

"All right," he said, "let's try it again." He clucked and flicked the reins and that served to get the horses' attention. He said "Hyah" in a subdued voice. The horses had learned well. The leaders lunged forward and the swing horses started out east and west and the wheelers jumped, one of them getting a leg over the tongue and whinnying in panic until Lucky got down and helped him back into position. On the next try four horses leaned forward and Lucky grinned when the coach began to move, but the leaders had stood still, so there was a whinnying, protesting pileup that took a while to untangle.

A half-moon came up, lit the scene, and would have made it possible for someone to see the sweat beading on Lucky's face. Time after time it looked as if the thing were going to work, and then the horses got independent and the coach rolled to a stop with six animals tangled in the harness and looking walleyed at Lucky, but he was going to get the stage rolling if it took all night.

After one particularly bad tangle, with one horse on the ground threatening to break harness, Lucky looked up at the moon beseechingly and wondered if Maddy's spirit would forgive him if he reverted to old habits and turned the air a little blue. He got the horse on its feet and the harness straightened out and climbed back into the box and hesitated. It wasn't that he was a defeatist, it was just that he dreaded another tangle and he needed a little blow before he tried again. He didn't hear anyone approach and knew that he wasn't alone only when the body of the stage rocked on the thoroughbrace and Bowen Lockhart climbed onto the seat beside him.

Enough time had passed for Bowen's beard to flower again and for his hair to grow a bit. He was as ragged as ever and smelled strongly of scotch whiskey.

"Evening, Bowen," Lucky said.

"I've been watching," Bowen said. He took the reins out of Lucky's hands. Lucky didn't protest. He could see in the moonlight that Bowen was bunching three reins in one hand, three in the others. Then he put all six in one hand and picked up the whip and said "Hyah" just as the whip snapped an inch or two over the ears of the leaders, and then the reins were in their proper hands and one hand moved to slap reins on the rump of the reluctant gee side wheeler. With a jerk and a muted rumble of wheels, the Dos Caballos Stage Company started to roll.

"How'd you do that?" Lucky asked.

"Watch," Bowen said, pulling the coach to a halt and then doing it again.

"Where'd you learn to drive a stage?" Lucky asked.

"Didn't," Bowen said.

"Then how come you can and I can't?"

"Done some four-in-hand. Six-in-hand isn't much different."

All of which didn't help Lucky a lot. Bowen drove the coach at an easy walk out of town and onto the road leading down the hill. He stopped the coach and handed Lucky the reins, positioning the reins just right, using his own hands when Lucky didn't pull right. In a couple of hours Lucky was starting and stopping and turning in a short circle down near the creek.

"One must be more intelligent than the beasts," Bowen said when Lucky got the horses tangled on a turn.

Lucky said, "Well, dadgum it, I'm trying to be."

By sunup Lucky had the hang of it. They'd driven a couple of miles from town, and after Bowen had proved that it wasn't disastrous, Lucky coaxed the six horses into a rolling run and couldn't resist giving one "Woo-ha" whoop as the dust flowered up behind them in the moonlight.

Lucky let Bowen off at the Dos Caballos. The town was not yet stirring as Bowen got on his horse and headed for his hut in the hills. Lucky took the coach back down the road a mile or so and let the horses rest a bit until he was sure the town was awake. Then he yelped the team into motion, goaded them into a mile-covering run, and went bumping and thundering into Dos Caballos with the sun on his bare head and whooping at the top of his voice. He saw both Osa and Catalina run out onto the porch, and he wheeled the coach to a stop right in front of them, the horses digging in their heels with the suddenness of it.

When the dust settled, he saw that Catalina was looking at him with what he hoped was respect, and that Osa's mouth was open. "The Dos Caballos Stagecoach Company is now in business," he said. "The first trip to Socorro will leave tomorrow at sunup."

By the time word got around, Lucky had the horses unhitched, dried down, and in the corral. He walked down to the Dos Caballos to ask Osa how many had signed up for the trip. Osa glowered at him. "Exactly no one," Osa said.

"Well, we'll see about that," Lucky said. He started a round of the town, telling everyone that the stage was going to Socorro next morning, would spend one night there, and that there was plenty of space on top to carry back supplies. He'd never talked to so many busy people in his life. Suddenly everyone in Dos Caballos had something important to do. No one could get away right now to go to Socorro.

Heck Logan, who had stayed in town longer than he'd ever stayed to see what happened with Lucky and the coach, had the decency to explain, although it embarrassed him to do so. "It's your luck, boy," he said. "No one wants to ride with a man with your luck on them switchback roads through the mountains."

"I will go with Lucky," Catalina said when Lucky, a bit down in the mouth, went to the Dos Caballos Cantina.

"You will stay and watch the store," Osa said.

"You're going, then, Osa?" Lucky asked.

"I will stay and watch the store too."

"Well," Lucky said, "the stage is going if I have to ride it by myself."

He was saved from total humiliation when, that evening, Zelma Clemmons announced that since it was her twenty-fifth wedding anniversary, she and the mister were going to have a real celebration in Socorro. She turned and stared into Lucky's gray eyes. "And I'm going to be watching you every foot of the way, so you'd better be damned careful."

Lucky was up two hours before dawn, checking and rechecking. He had the horses hitched and ready before first light. He moved the stage onto the street and watched the sun come up, and then Zelma and a doubtful, quite reluctant Mack came walking down the street carrying one carpetbag each. He got a pretty good feeling when money changed hands, coming into the coffers of the Dos Caballos Stagecoach Company for the first time. He felt so good, he invited Mack and Zelma to ride up top with him, but Zelma said, "Hell, no, I'm paying full fare. We'll ride in comfort."

Lucky was in the seat, wondering if he remembered all that Bowen had taught him when Bowen himself came riding into town wearing fringed, clean buckskins, his beard neatly trimmed, a brace of ornate dueling pistols stuck in his belt, and an old Sharps rifle in hand. He unsaddled his horse and turned it into Lucky's corral and climbed up onto the seat.

"I have a yen," he said, "to do some drinking in civilized surroundings for a change."

"Well, I'm right grateful for the company," Lucky said.

The road in the immediate vicinity of the town was relatively smooth. The breeze of movement was pleasant in Lucky's face. It was only when the road began to climb out of the canyon that things got a little bit thrilling. On the first switchback, Lucky had the impulse to hand the reins to Bowen, but it was his coach, after all, and he'd have to do the driving in the future, so he might as well do it now. Bowen found it necessary only once to offer advice, when the road curved so sharply atop a hundred-foot drop that the horses had to go around the bend in teams of two and Lucky had to reach over with his outside hand to shorten the reins of the inside leaders, swing horses, and wheelers in turn. He sighed in relief and noted that Bowen looked a little more relaxed after he'd successfully negotiated a couple of more sharp turns.

There was a stretch of easy going as the road followed the stream once more through a pretty little canyon almost wide enough to be called a valley. Lucky was feeling good.

"Say, Bowen," he asked, "you plan to wear that Black Watch rig next year on the Queen's birthday?"

Bowen nodded. "I will always honor the Queen's birthday."

"You mind if I sell tickets, then?" Lucky asked.

"Have at it and I will take a split," Bowen said.

The wheels hissed through dry sand. The stream, nearby, sparkled in the sun. There was a smell of green, growing things in the air. Life, Lucky decided, was good. His only regret was that Osa had not had enough confidence in him to allow him to bring Catalina. Surely now that he was a solid businessman with his bad luck behind him, Osa must see that he would do as well for Catalina as some San Francisco city slicker. He was deep in his dreams, only idly looking ahead to the point where the road began to climb again to cross another hog's back when Bowen jerked his rifle up and tensed. Lucky saw them then, a dozen or so of them, Apache. They came out of the rocks and brush, six on one side, six on the other.

"Hold on," Lucky said, "it's just Nana and some of his boys." He pulled the horses to a halt and they seemed to be not displeased about having a chance to rest.

"*Buenas dias,* Nana," he said, speaking in Spanish, "so you have returned from Mexico."

Nana was a boy, not more than sixteen, son of the regional chief. The old chief enjoyed his comfort now and was gradually turning over leadership to his son. Most of the time the Fray Cristobals were empty of Indians, since they preferred the better hunting grounds to the west, coupled with the occasional fun raid into Mexico for women and horses. Nana was well known to the residents of Dos Caballos. There existed between Apache and the few Spanish and American whites who lived in and around the town a sort of tacit understanding: Don't bother us and we won't bother you.

"I will see this shining wickiup on wheels," Nana said, dismounting.

Zelma Clemmons threw open the stagecoach door and called out a greeting to the young chief. Nana beamed at her, quite un-Apachelike, and climbed in to sit beside her, pounding the leather seats, running his fingers over the polished wood. The other Apache warriors examined the coach from the outside, trying to see their reflections in the polished brass.

After a thorough and delighted examination of the interior, Nana leapt lightly to the ground and clambered atop the coach, standing there with a broad smile on his round, dark face. He wore once-white Mexican breeches tucked into leather leggings, a belt from which fell the traditional kiltlike skirt. His mass of dark, sweat-wet hair was shoulder length and held back from his face with a headband. His torso was muscular for one so young.

"We have returned from Mexico with many good things," he said, not looking at anyone but obviously answering Lucky's previous remark.

"So . . ." Lucky responded. There hadn't been any problems with the Chiricahua since he'd arrived in Dos Caballos, but an Apache was an Apache. War was a business with the Chiricahua. Fortunately they found the pickings to be richer in Mexico. He knew that Nana had been trained from the time he was a small boy to fight, to raid with minimum risk in search of booty and women. Once he'd seen Nana training with other young men, dodging arrows shot at them from a deadly range. An Apache warrior like Nana could run miles in the heat of summer with a mouthful of water and spit it out at the end to show, disdainfully, that he wasn't thirsty. The Apache and the Navajo had been very involved in driving the Spaniards from the New Mexico Territory not too long in the past, and the Apache was not a fellow to toy with.

"I will give you twenty Mexican horses, all of good blood, for this shining wickiup on wheels," Nana said.

"So you like the stagecoach," Lucky said.

"I like," Nana said. "The horses are fresh, well fed. You can sell them in Socorro for much gold."

"Well, Nana," Lucky said, "I appreciate that you like the stagecoach, but it belongs to the Dos Caballos Stagecoach Company. It will make regular runs down to Socorro and back. Sometimes, if you like, we can bring back supplies for you and your tribe on the coach."

"We also brought from Mexico two beautiful young girls," Nana said, his smile fading. "They have been well treated. They are virgins and free of troublesome disease."

Bowen snorted. Lucky didn't think the statements very likely in view of the smug looks on the faces of Nana's warriors.

"In addition," Nana said, "I will give you a freshly killed antelope so that you may eat fresh meat."

"Nana," Lucky said, "I wish I could accommodate you. Look, this coach just wouldn't go where you want to go. It has to have a road. It would not be good for the Apache. And besides, it belongs to the Dos Caballos Stagecoach Company and is not for trade."

"My spirit man hungers for it," Nana said, his face clouding.

"We are friends, the people of Dos Caballos and the Chiricahua of Nana's father," Lucky said. "Let us remain friends."

Nana leapt from the coach. Beside Lucky, Bowen Lockhart followed the movement with his rifle. The young Apache's face showed his anger. "You will not trade the shining wickiup on wheels even though I offer twenty horses, two beautiful Mexican virgins, and a freshly killed antelope?"

"I'm sorry, Nana, but no," Lucky said.

Nana turned and spoke to his warriors, who had grouped themselves behind him.

"Lucky," Mack Clemmons said from inside, "he just told his braves to take the coach."

Bowen stood in the driver's seat, pointed the big, ugly Sharps right at Nana's face. "I do not speak the language," he said, "so will you please tell this young man that he will be the first to die."

"What does the white man say?" Nana asked sullenly.

"He says he's going to kill you," Lucky said. "He says if you try to take this coach, you'll be the first to die. You've seen me shoot my Sharps, Nana. You've seen the hole it makes in a deer."

Nana's face went tense, then stoic. "Indeed," he said, "the Chiricahua and the white men of Dos Caballos have always been friends."

"Good," Lucky said. He hyahed the horses into motion. The Apache watched the coach go, did not mount their horses until the stage had climbed out of the canyon and disappeared around a switchback.

"Will they follow?" Bowen asked.

Lucky shook his head. "It's Nana's spirit man that worries me. That was his way of saying that he wanted this coach real bad. When the spirit man hungers in an Apache, watch out."

It pleased Lucky to reach the Rio Grande in one day's run without lathering the horses too much. Zelma took over the woman's work of cooking beans, biscuits, and coffee. Lucky cooled the horses and rubbed them down. Mack came up with a bottle of Osa's unwatered whiskey, and while Bowen watched and listened just in case Nana's spirit man had overcome a boy's natural reluctance to be punctured with a big piece of lead, Zelma and Mack sang, rather sweetly, a plaintive, old English folk ballad that had been taught to Mack by his mother way back in New York State before she died and left Mack with nothing to do but start traveling west.

A stagecoach coming into a small western town always attracted attention. The Dos Caballos stage, coming into Socorro from the south, drew a crowd of ragtag boys and the eyes of all. Lucky didn't showboat it. He came in slow and easy. The horses had had a long pull and they got his attention first, while Zelma and Mack went off to the hotel to begin their celebration. Bowen, wiping his lips with the back of his hand in anticipation, headed for a saloon.

Lucky had just turned the horses into stalls in the stable with some fresh hay and a bit of corn and was making a close examination of the coach to see how it had weathered the first run when he looked up to see the cold-faced, warm-eyed personage of Chunk Wilson. Wilson was standing, feet spread, one hand holding a cigar in front of his face.

"Where in hell did you get a stagecoach?" Wilson demanded.

Lucky stood up straight and looked Wilson in the eye. "Why would that concern you, Mr. Wilson?" he asked in a pleasant tone of voice. He was enjoying his moment. They'd laughed at him for suggesting that Wilson run a coach up to Dos Caballos now and then. Now it was his turn to laugh, because Dos Caballos had its own stage line.

Wilson's voice changed to a more congenial tone. "Just curious," he said. "Dos Caballos Stage Company, is it?"

"That's right," Lucky said, using his sleeve to polish the neatly painted letters on the door. "Says so right here."

"Good-looking rig. Old model."

"Maybe," Lucky said.

"You've done a lot of repair, I see."

"Quite a bit," Lucky said.

"Gonna make regular runs, huh?"

"That's the idea," Lucky said.

"Hmm," Wilson said. "I'd still like to know where you got the coach."

Since Wilson was speaking civilly, Lucky saw no harm in telling him. "Well, I ran into it one day when I got lost in the mountains. It was a mess."

"This stage belonged to the Butterworth Overland," Wilson said.

"Oh?" Lucky said, interested. "How do you know that, Mr. Wilson?"

"Because there's never been a stagecoach in New Mexico that didn't belong to Butterworth," Wilson said. "And I bought all of the Butterworth rolling stock and equipment."

Lucky began to get a bit uneasy. "Well, I don't see how you could have bought this one, Mr. Wilson, since it's been lying at the bottom of a brush canyon for a lot of years. I'd say a long time before the Overland Mail started coming through New Mexico."

"I'll tell you what I'm going to do," Wilson said. "You've done a lot of fine work here. And they tell me you bought six pretty good horses from Spud Shank, up the river. I'm going to give you a thousand dollars for the whole rig."

For a moment that sounded pretty good to Lucky. He'd be able to give back Osa's five hundred and they'd have two hundred and fifty apiece, which happened to be more money than Lucky had ever had at one time in his life. Then he remembered the way Catalina had looked at him the day he came roaring up in front of the Dos Caballos.

"Mr. Wilson," he said, "that sounds like a mighty fine offer, and I thank you for it. But you see, there's a lot of folks up in Dos Caballos who are real proud to have a stage line coming in. It'll give them a way to get down the mountains and carry in supplies, and it gives the town a little prestige."

"Smith, I can take this coach, you know," Wilson said.

Lucky felt his face freeze and his eyes began to narrow a little. "Well, I reckon you could try, Mr. Wilson."

Wilson shrugged. "Hell, it's not worth killing over. Old as it is, it'll fall apart. I'll tell you this, though. I've got a contract with the U.S. government, giving me sole right to operate stage lines in New Mexico Territory. Now you know and I know that you're not going to be doing enough business to hurt me, but I can't have it. Let one two-bit operator like you get away with it, and who knows who would begin to get big ideas. You've got two choices, Smith. My offer of a thousand will hold until tomorrow."

"What's the other choice?" Lucky asked stiffly.

Wilson grinned under his drooping mustache. "Now, would a man incriminate himself by telling a very unlucky fellow what's going to happen to him if he doesn't use good sense?"

Chapter Seven

The first scheduled run of the Dos Caballos Stagecoach Line had reached Socorro just after five o'clock on a fine July afternoon. The heat had only begun to moderate slightly from its mid-afternoon high. Bowen Lockhart had accumulated some dust, and he stood beside the coach trying to brush a couple of pounds of it off his buckskins. The skins were infernally hot. He was reasonably sure that about two gallons of cold beer would help. He left his Sharps inside the coach, put the dueling pistols under the driver's seat, and started walking toward the nearest saloon.

He stepped up from the dust of the street onto a boardwalk, stomped his boots to loosen dust, pushed his hat back, and grinned in anticipation. There were only a few people abroad in the heat of the afternoon. A prospector was coming down the street, walking slow, his donkey following without a lead. A storekeeper in vest and shirt sleeves was standing outside his door, a straw in his mouth, arms crossed over his chest. A group of dusty-looking ranch hands leaned against the front wall of the saloon. On the other side of the saloon door, farthest away from Bowen as he approached, a tall, slim, mean-faced man in black, a heavy Colt on his thigh, was watching the approach of two well-dressed young people, obviously Easterners, walking side by side down the boardwalk.

Bowen wasn't being too observant. He was thinking maybe that after he drank about a gallon of beer he'd pour another gallon down the neck of his buckskins to cool off the outer body as well as the inner man. He was nearing the door, walking past the group of ranch hands, when the man in black pushed himself away from the wall and put himself directly in front of the well-dressed young couple. Bowen couldn't hear what the man said, and he didn't much care. He looked once, saw a well-coiffed head of auburn hair on the girl, saw her jerk her arm away from the man in black and say something with a look of cool contempt on her face. He did hear the young man's words.

"I must ask you, sir, to stop bothering the lady," the young man said, the accent halting Bowen in his tracks.

It happened quite quickly then. The man in black swung, and the well-dressed young man took the blow directly on the chin and went down heavily. The man in black seized the young girl by both arms. He was laughing. Bowen was moving as the girl tried unsuccessfully to kick the man in the groin.

The ranch hands were looking on with impassive interest.

The girl was now struggling in her accoster's arms, jerking her face to right and left, not crying out, to avoid his kiss. Bowen tapped the man in black on the shoulder. The man turned, a snarl on his face, and the snarl was wiped off by Bowen's hard left. The girl jerked away as the man in black fell to roll off the boardwalk and thud to the dirt street, raising a small cloud of dust.

If anyone who knew Bowen had been there, they would have seen a new look on his face, a look of softness, of something undefined, as he bowed to the young lady and then bent to put his hands under the boy—for the fallen man was quite young—and help him to his unsteady feet.

"Have I not told you, time and time again, that there is a time for talking and yet another time for fighting?" Bowen demanded. "Words will neither prevent nor win a fight."

The boy's eyes focused. Bowen's words made him shake his head, and then he was staring, openmouthed. "Are ye, then, Bowen Lockhart?" he asked.

"This?" the young girl exclaimed. "This is our father?"

* * *

Lucky just managed to catch the Socorro postmaster before closing and was handed a very official-looking envelope from Washington, D.C. His hands trembled just a little as he opened it. Then he whooped and showed the letter to the postmaster. The postmaster smiled thinly.

"Well, young man," he said, "you are now the holder of a United States contract to deliver the United States mail to Dos Caballos. Congratulations."

Since no one had been down to Socorro lately, there was an accumulation of mail: three letters and one small package for the Widow Brown from her sister in St. Louis. Lucky felt good as he carried the mail, quite officially, out of the post office. He saw the postmaster leave behind him but didn't watch to see the man half run across the street to the Socorro Saloon, where within three minutes he was reporting the latest development to Chunk Wilson.

Lucky was looking for a lawyer. He was going over Chunk's words in his mind, and there was enough doubt to quickly cool his pleasure over the mail contract. If, indeed, the law said Wilson owned New Mexico Territory as far as stage service was concerned, then he'd have no choice but to sell out to Wilson.

Socorro's one lawyer lived and worked in the same two rooms at the end of the street. It was no trouble to locate him. He didn't seem to be too eager to talk. Lucky was trail-worn and dusty, and the likes of such, the lawyer knew, seldom had any cash money. But when Lucky mentioned his ownership of a stagecoach line, he had the lawyer's attention. Lucky shelled out five dollars of Osa's money as a retainer and told his story.

"And you say the United States Post Office has given you a mail contract?" the lawyer asked. Lucky handed over the letter and waited. "Hmm," the lawyer said, "one must not make assumptions, but it seems likely to me, my friend, that the United States Post Office would have checked to see if issuing this contract infringed on any other contracts."

"Sounds reasonable," Lucky said. "I guess the United States Post Office knows what it's doing."

"Actually," the lawyer said, "I can't give you an opinion until I've seen Mr. Wilson's contracts. Then we can decide what to do."

"I wonder if you could shake a leg on that," Lucky said, remembering that Wilson's buy-out offer was limited in time.

"I'm quite busy," the lawyer said. Lucky looked around, saw cobwebs in the corner, dust on papers scattered over the lawyer's desk. "But," the lawyer added quickly, "I think I can get to that tomorrow."

Lucky went out in search of Bowen, heading toward the saloon nearest the stable. The coach was sitting in front of the stable, gleaming in the sunset. He didn't see Bowen in the saloon. He didn't go in, and he told himself that he was not being cowardly, just smart. Now was not the time to run afoul of Chunk Wilson's men. He checked another saloon, saw Chunk Wilson at the bar, saw the man he'd fought with, Craw Maddock, leaning back against the bar telling all and sundry what he was going to do to the dude who had coldcocked him from behind when he found him.

Lucky checked the hotel dining room, found Mack and Zelma Clemmons, but no Bowen. He used some of the fare money—a man had to have a salary if he was going to work—to buy a big, pan-fried steak and a pile of fried potatoes and listened to Zelma Clemmons reminiscing about how she'd met Mack back in Independence. When Lucky got around to asking the Clemmonses if they'd seen Bowen, he was surprised to learn that, yes, Bowen had passed through the lobby with a handsome young couple on the way upstairs.

Chunk Wilson had pulled Craw Maddock off to a quiet corner. "I thought you liked working for me," Wilson demanded.

"Sure," Maddock said, puzzled.

"Then keep your damned mouth shut. I don't want you getting involved in a gunfight right now. I'll probably have an important job for you after tomorrow."

Maddock said, "Damn, Mr. Wilson, that bastard from Dos Caballos snuck up on me from behind and coldcocked me. You expect me to let him get away with that?"

"He was from Dos Caballos?"

"Come in on the stage with that Lucky feller," Maddock said.

"All right," Wilson said. "But there'll be a time for that. Right now I want you to stay sober and stand by to ride when I tell you to. You got that?"

"I don't take kindly to it, letting that bastard get by with backstabbing me," Maddock said coldly.

Wilson's eyes grew, if anything, even warmer, but his voice was icy. "Tell you what, Craw, anytime you think you're smart enough"—he pushed back his coat to reveal the butt of a .44—"or fast enough to be the boss, you just let me know."

Maddock's face flushed, then he subsided. "No offense, Mr. Wilson."

"None taken—yet," Wilson said.

Cameron Lockhart was angry. He'd been angry ever since his mother had been stabbed with a pair of scissors by the jealous wife of one of her lovers. He'd started being angry then because the scandal had proven to him, against his wishes and his long-standing beliefs, that his father may just have been partially justified in leaving the Lockhart estate near Peterhead in Scotland, and that perhaps Bowen Lockhart had other reasons for leaving than a desire to get out of one of Scotland's starkest districts. He'd been angry all the way across the Atlantic because he had had no desire to go journeying away from what was rightfully his but couldn't be his legally as long as there was a chance that his father was alive.

Cameron was as tall as his father but not as bulky. He was solidly built, but he had the face of a boy. Any stranger would have underestimated his twenty-two years by at least four, most often by more. He had not seen his father since his twelfth birthday, when Bowen had first given him a pony and cart and then the dubious gift of his absence.

Cara Lockhart remembered little of her father, since she'd been only five when he disappeared. There'd been pictures, of course. She had salvaged them from the garbage where her mother had tossed them and had kept them hidden in her own rooms all those years. She had always thought that her father must have been the most handsome man in Scotland, especially when he was in uniform. Now, at seventeen, she was a bit shy in his presence, and when, in her own room in the hotel—it was larger than Cameron's—he took her hand and looked into the blue eyes that she'd taken from him and said, "Darling girl, how I have missed you," she didn't know how to react.

There had been quite a fight with her brother when she'd insisted on accompanying him to the New World to find whether Bowen Lockhart was dead or alive, but as her mother had often told her, not kindly in most instances, she had her father's stubbornness, and she'd prevailed. In fact, her patience and her desire to see the man she could remember only vaguely—big, smelling of Scotch whiskey, with a beard that scratched her face when he kissed her—had kept them going when it seemed that there was no purpose in going on. The last letter from Bowen Lockhart had come from some godforsaken little town in New Mexico Territory a full five years in the past, and it had been difficult to find anyone who knew where Socorro was, much less how to get there.

The getting there had been rather exciting, at least to Cara. Cameron had carried his small pistol all the way from St. Louis, just in case highwaymen ambushed the various stagecoaches on which they'd ridden. Cameron had cursed the dust and the distances and the hardness of the seats. Cara had been agog at the vast, sweeping landscape, the color and charm of the hardy folks who'd dared to settle the American West, the romance of the noble Indians they saw along the way.

Stagecoaches pictured in Eastern publications were always moving at a gallop. Cara and Cameron found that in actuality there was not all that much galloping, that hundreds and hundreds of miles of slowly varying landscape passed by the windows at an average speed of five and a half miles an hour, and that that pace was held day and night, rain, sun, or storm. One had to catch a miserable little nap while being jostled around, usually crowded against some stranger. Some good and some rather abominable meals had been taken at home stations, and one had to train one's bodily systems to wait patiently for a stop at a change station, every eight or ten miles in rough country, up to twenty-five miles where the roads were better.

Through it all Cara had maintained, for the most part, her sense of high adventure, often to Cameron's total disgust. And then, upon arriving in Socorro, from which point Bowen's last letter had originated, addressed to Cameron, they had been unable to find anyone who had ever heard of a Scotsman named Lockhart. Over Cara's objection, Cameron had been discussing the possibility of a faked death certificate when they were accosted on the board sidewalk by Craw Maddock.

"I cannot believe you've flowered into such a striking woman," Bowen said, kissing Cara on the cheek only after they were in the privacy of her room, with Cameron glowering and looking on disapprovingly. "And you, lad, ah, you're a Lockhart, all right." He pounded Cameron on the shoulder and Cameron moved away.

"Mother is dead," Cameron said.

"Ah, and that's too bad," Bowen said. "She was not a bad woman, not actually."

"Aren't you going to ask how?" Cameron asked belligerently.

"No," Bowen said. "Do ye care to tell me?"

"No," Cameron said sharply.

"Well, then."

"We're here for one reason," Cameron said. "The courts will not give me full control of the estates as long as you're alive."

"Well, then, that's easily solved," Bowen said calmly. "Lend me your pistol and I shall shoot myself forthwith."

Cara giggled.

"But perhaps we can solve the problem in a less painful way for me," Bowen said. "Must we talk of business now, this minute? I have grieved for being away from you, my children. Ye may not believe that, Cameron, but it is true."

Cameron felt a brief softening but resisted it. "There is another way," he said. "A signed and witnessed document that you absolve yourself of all interest in the Lockhart estates in my favor."

"Ye shall have it," Bowen said. "And the McCann estates, those of your mother?"

"They are already mine," Cameron said. "She saw to that."

"Good for her," Bowen said. "That's it, then. We shall draw up the papers tomorrow, if that's soon enough for you." He rubbed his hands together. "Do ye take from the Lockhart side in a liking for good whiskey, lad?"

"I don't drink," Cameron said stiffly.

"A shame," Bowen said.

"I do," Cara said.

"She does not, and she *will* not," Cameron shouted, and the Scot's accent on the words, the soft burr, made Bowen sentimental. He turned to Cara.

"Since you have come so far away, Daughter, I would like to have just a wee bit of time to get to know you. Can you not stay for a while?"

"Yes," Cara said.

"No," Cameron said.

"Can we not have a civilized dinner, below in the dining room, and talk, then?" Bowen asked.

Bowen could not keep his eyes off his daughter's animated face. They carried on conversation over dinner, after he'd introduced both Cameron and Cara to an astounded group of Dos Caballos stage passengers just finishing up their meal. He saw in her his own likeness—his eyes, his mouth—and the slim, proud beauty of the woman he'd married, the woman who had immediately set out to dominate his life in every way, to force him to give up his one love, soldiering, to be at her beck and call day and night and, failing in that, to strike out at him in the way that she knew would hurt most—by giving her slim, lovely body to other men. He had suspected and had not the courage to face it, lying to himself. She had hinted and he had ignored. And then she'd seen to it that she was discovered, slim body gleaming with perspiration, heaving, with one of Bowen's fellow officers. He had fought against a natural urge to kill both, and then he'd left.

"Cameron," Cara said after a long, lovely time of eating and talking with her father, of finding that she did, after all, remember how she'd loved him, how she'd thrilled each time he came home to lift her high and swing her and call her his bonny lass, "I am not leaving on the next stage. If you must go, go."

"I cannot leave ye alone in this wilderness," Cameron protested.

"I will not be alone," she said.

She turned to her father. "Tell me about Dos Caballos."

"In a way it is like Scotland," he said. "Barren, lonely, and peopled by odd folk, but dry."

"I think I'm going to love it," she said.

"Oh, I don't think you'll love it. The starkness of the mountains might interest you. Below my hut the stream runs into a deep pool for swimming, and I catch great, hulking trout there."

"Lovely," Cara said. "Cameron, please?"

"Oh, all right, then," Cameron said. "A week, no more."

To his delight, the Socorro lawyer had two clients the next day. First, even before he'd had time to drink his breakfast, three Scots and a rather simple legal paper that required only the signature of the local justice of the peace, then Lucky Smith.

"Mr. Smith," the lawyer said, "I have been able to read the legal documents pertaining to Mr. Wilson's rights in the territory, and I have good news and bad news for you. The good news is that there is nothing in Mr. Wilson's contracts with the U.S. government to preclude small, independent spur lines such as yours."

"I appreciate your work," Lucky said.

"The bad news comes from the mouth of Mr. Wilson, himself, and I quote," the lawyer said. "He said, 'Mr. Sykes, you have my permission to tell Mr. Smith that my offer of a buy-out is withdrawn at sundown today and that if he doesn't take it, he will be coyote meat before another sundown.' "

"I appreciate your telling me," Lucky said, gray eyes squinting just a little.

"I've only just met you," Sykes said, "so it is presumptuous to give advice outside the legal arena, but I would think, Mr. Smith, that it might be wise to accept Mr. Wilson's offer. Although you seem to have the legal right to operate a coach between Dos Caballos and Socorro, there is another matter—the ownership of the coach itself."

"I found that coach wrecked in the mountains," Lucky said. "If I hadn't cut a mile of brush and hauled the pieces out and put them back together, it'd still be dry-rotting up in the hills."

"Still," Sykes said, "if, as Mr. Wilson claims, the coach was originally the property of the Butterworth interests, he has a legal claim to it, since he bought all the running stock."

"This one wasn't running," Lucky protested.

"At best," Sykes said, "he could stop you from operating until the question was settled by a court, and I hesitate to admit it, but I don't think you'd have much chance against a leading citizen like Mr. Wilson in any court in the territory."

Lucky rose. His gray eyes narrowed thoughtfully.

"It's a fair offer, Mr. Smith," Sykes said.

"Yes," Lucky said, "I guess it is. But then it's not so much an offer as it is a demand, is it?"

When Cara came down for breakfast, Bowen was seated alone at a table. He leapt to his feet, smiling broadly. It had been a long time since anything had given him the pleasure he experienced looking at his daughter. He had cleaned up his buckskins with a wet rag, and he'd brushed his hair carefully after shaving. Cara thought that he was quite handsome, that he could have posed for an artist as a fine example of the Western pioneer.

Cara, too, smiled in pleasure, and then her smile faded into guilt as she thought of her mother. She had had her suspicions that her dear mother liked not only her wee nip but other pleasures requiring the presence of a male. Her mother had had no kind words for the memory of Bowen Lockhart, but she'd loved her mother very much, and it now seemed disloyal to her mother's memory to feel the way she felt about this handsome man, who was her father and a stranger at the same time. But it was a lovely day and everyone had his faults. She was beginning to understand that her mother had had her own faults, and she was sure, without dwelling on it at the moment, that her father could have found a solution other than disappearing from the face of the earth. So perhaps the fault of one canceled out the fault of the other. She knew only that she was young and vibrantly alive, and that she'd experienced many adventures, with more ahead. Moreover, she *liked* her father. She'd lost her mother, so she saw no reason to give up a newly rediscovered father simply because he and her mother had found it impossible to live together.

She kissed Bowen on the forehead and sat down. The friendly, rather fat matron who ran the hotel dining room hovered over her, giving off aromas of cooking grease and flour, and suggested a breakfast so hearty that Cara gasped before realizing that she was indeed famished.

"Through the night," Bowen said, "I have had time to think, Daughter. This New Mexico is a rugged land, and no place for a lady. I will stay in Socorro for a few days so that you and I and the lad can get reacquainted."

"But we were going to Dos Caballos," Cara said.

"It is a long, hot, dusty trip." He was thinking of his hot, dusty, littered adobe shack, and he couldn't see this beautiful Scottish flower at home in it, not even temporarily. "I see no reason to expose you to such hardship."

"I've ridden stages for hundreds of miles," she said. "I have made up my mind, and you know that we Lockharts are stubborn."

So Bowen decided he could put his son and daughter up at the Widow Brown's boardinghouse. At least the food was good there, and they must have seen worse surroundings on the trip west.

"Mother was killed by the wife of her lover," Cara said, face down, a blush spreading over her peaches-and-cream cheeks.

"Ah, you poor thing," Bowen said, taking her hand.

"For a long time I hated you for leaving me," she said.

"Ah," he said, wondering if the tears were going to come and embarrass him.

"I think I understand now." She looked at him, and he knew that one day a man was going to drown in those deep blue eyes. "You loved her very much, didn't you?"

It was a moment before Bowen could speak. He did have to wipe tears with the back of one rough hand. "You are more than I deserve, my Cara," he whispered. "A lass of surpassing understanding."

"Well," she said, bouncing up, trying to hide her own tears, "I must finish my packing, for I am eager to see this Dos Caballos of yours."

Chapter Eight

No newspaperman worthy of the name would have missed chronicling an event so momentous as the establishment of a new stage line to Socorro. The consumptive, hard-drinking editor of the Socorro *Perspectiva* caught Lucky as he was harnessing the team for the return trip to Dos Caballos. The coach was two days gone from Socorro before the *Perspectiva* came rattling off the press and was available for circulation. The editor, Botts, enjoyed writing and printing the paper; getting it into the hands of the reader interested him little, so that distribution was a do-it-yourself project on the part of the curious. It was another full day before Craw Maddock carried a copy into Wilson's office.

Maddock, himself, couldn't make out all the fancy words, but a storekeeper who had managed to keep a straight face had pointed out a front-page article extolling the healthful air and charming quaintness of Socorro's neighboring village in the mountains.

Maddock sat perched on the edge of Wilson's desk while Chunk scanned the small, crowded, bleeding print with one eye squinted against an upflow of cigar smoke. Finished, Wilson threw the paper violently to the floor.

"Reckon that Lucky feller's gonna take over the whole shebang?"

Maddock asked dryly. That was a repeat of a question from one of the boys in the saloon.

"Now, Craw," Wilson said, having recovered from his momentary loss of poise, "you just don't appreciate good writing. Why, old Botts has outdone himself. He used this historic event as a springboard to write rapturously of the entire history of transportation in New Mexico. Or did you read that part?"

"I didn't read it too close," Maddock said, looking away.

"Now, I fancy that young Lucky Smith, when he has a chance to read this piece of great American literature, will see himself in the company of the glorious Mr. McKnight, who made the first attempt to carry goods into this territory in 1811, and was rewarded by the Spanish by being tossed into the *calabozo;* and with those hardy pioneers who came in Pittsburgh wagons to trade in Santa Fe, almost a two-thousand-mile round trip."

"Huh?" Maddock said.

"You don't agree that our friend, Smith, is a heroic young man?"

"Naw," Maddock said.

"Nor do I, goddammit," Wilson shouted, jerking his cigar out of his mouth and leaping to his feet. "I want you to go down and see Mr. Editor Botts and tell him that I'm slightly disappointed in him, what with me spending good money to advertise in his paper, giving all this space to a coach line that won't be in operation when the next issue of his paper comes out, running off at the mouth about the beauty of a one-horse town in the mountains."

"Can't call it a one-horse town," Maddock said, grinning.

"Get out of here," Wilson said.

" 'Cause it's name is two horses," Maddock said, still grinning as he ducked out the door.

Botts's newspaper story would not find its way to Dos Caballos for a while. The stage had made the return trip, carrying its first incoming passengers, to the pleasure of Osa and the potential downfall of his daughter, and to the interest of everyone else.

Cara had thoroughly enjoyed the trip. When the going was relatively smooth, she sat on top with Lucky and her father and was able to see the occasional small animal, and a landscape that seemed to be huge enough to overwhelm her totally. Her first sight of Dos Caballos was somewhat of a disappointment. She thought that the little village might be similar to some she'd read about in exciting books about India but didn't voice that opinion lest she be considered either imaginative or stupid.

A small gathering, including Osa and Catalina, greeted the return. Osa pulled Lucky aside quickly, after learning that the passengers were Bowen Lockhart's son and daughter, to ask Lucky if they were paying passengers. He smiled when Lucky assured him that Bowen had paid with good silver.

Cameron had ridden in what comfort the interior of the coach offered, finding himself interested in spite of himself in Mack Clennons's accounts of almost finding a mother lode not once but several times. When he stepped down onto the dusty street of Dos Caballos, he looked around with predisposed disgust and into the eyes of the most striking girl he'd ever seen.

When Cameron's blue eyes locked onto the deep, dark Spanish eyes of Osa's treasured daughter, the whole world went dizzy for a moment for Catalina. Although no male hand had been more intimate than a quick, passing pat on her well-skirted and petticoated fanny, and her lips had yet to know the feel of kissed passion, Catalina's experience in the cantina had made her, she would have said, quite knowledgeable about men. But she'd never seen a man like Cameron Lockhart. His curly blond locks fell so prettily over his ears. His blue eyes had the spirit of the sea, which she'd never seen. He was by far the most beautiful man she'd ever seen, and for long moments she let him penetrate, invade, possess her own eyes, and through them her soul. Then she jerked her head, looked away, and called out a gay greeting to Lucky.

"Come," Osa bellowed happily, "to celebrate the first visitors to our fair city the drinks—just the first one, mind you—are on Osa Carranza."

"Please, let's do," Cara begged Bowen when he started to pull her away toward the boardinghouse.

There was no doubt that Cameron would go. He was unable to take his eyes off the sultry beauty of Catalina, so all and sundry adjourned from the open air to the old-beer and dead-cigar smell of the cantina. Catalina was so subdued that Osa kept looking at her, wondering what was wrong. When she served the Lockharts' table, she curtsied politely and smiled like a shy child.

Lucky, having finished rubbing down the horses and smelling quite loudly of them, ducked into the cantina, brushed dust off onto the dirt floor, and looked for Catalina. He soon saw that she had eyes only for Cameron Lockhart and was indeed hovering over the Lockhart table. His feeling of well-being vanished, so that by the time he'd finished the free beer—there'd been a lively discussion with Osa as to the good business sense of giving one on the house to a business partner, as opposed to paying customers like the Clemmonses and the Lockharts—he felt about as rotten as buzzard droppings. He left quietly and didn't hear when Cara turned, looked all around, and asked, "Why, where's Mr. Smith?"

Osa woke early the next morning. He walked out into the crystalline air and felt pretty good until he looked up the street and saw six horses, plus Jughead and Coaly, in the corral and realized that it was all going to be outgo, for horses ate every day, until the stage made another run to Socorro. He saw Bowen Lockhart and his son come out of the boardinghouse and go down to the stable, then emerge a little later with Bowen riding his mare and Cameron aboard Lucky's old Jughead. He had not been blind to Catalina's fascination with the young Scot who dressed in a tweed suit that was much too hot for New Mexico, and he mused on what it all meant as the two men disappeared in the direction of the northern hills.

Bowen had two motives for dragging his son out so early. First of all, he just wanted to have a chance to talk with Cameron in privacy. Secondly—and this was quite natural, for he was, after all, only human—he had an almost unrealized urge to show his son that the old man wasn't just a desert rat in some sort of masochistic self-exile in a place created and promptly forgotten by God.

The ride was a long one and, for Cameron, an interesting one. The treed slopes were unlike anything in Scotland. The warming morning with its low humidity that seemed to make the very air sparkle was a tonic to him. They rode in silence for the most part, except when Bowen pointed out something of interest, or what he thought would be of interest to a lad just over from the Old Country.

It was three hours later when Cameron said, "Are we not riding around in circles?"

"Ye might say that," Bowen said. "I must be sure we are not followed, you know."

Cameron didn't understand and wondered if the solitude and the years of wandering had affected his father's brain. When Bowen led the way into a little box canyon, keeping the horses carefully on bare rock so as not to leave tracks, he was wishing that he'd stayed back in Dos Caballos to convince Cara that it was time to go home.

At the end of the canyon, hidden in brush, there was a low adobe hut. They left the horses there, hobbled, to find a bit of graze if they were exceptionally talented in searching out the sparse clumps of grass, and hiked a quarter mile to a point where a tiny rill cascaded down from the canyon's rim. Once, Cameron realized, there'd been a more impressive waterfall there, far back in time when rain was more plentiful in the region. There was still a pool of clear water at the foot of the falls.

It was, all in all, a pretty setting, and Cameron wondered why, if Bowen insisted on living so far out in the wilderness, he hadn't set up his house near the falls and the sweet water. He soon found out. The entrance to the mine was concealed well in brush, near the falls. There was a feeling of weight over his head as Cameron followed Bowen by lantern light deep into the canyon wall.

"I think you'll understand, Cameron," Bowen said, reaching a little chamber and putting down his lantern, "why I was going to be leaving this place soon."

Cameron just wanted to get back into the open air.

Bowen began to move a pile of stone and then pulled out an ironbound chest from a recess in the stone curtain of the shaft. He opened the top. Cameron peered in and saw small leather bags, the chest almost filled with them.

"I think I've just about exhausted the pocket," Cameron said, "but no doubt you'll agree that it was worthwhile."

Each bag contained gold in the form of dust, small grains, and some nuggets. The chest was so heavy that Bowen could barely slide it along the rock floor.

"The nuggets came from the stream," Bowen said, "as did some of the dust and grains. Some came from one vein here in the old Spanish mine. They had missed the vein by inches. I found it when a wall caved in and almost did for me. Used the stream's water and a rocker box to separate it from the matrix rock. Hard work, I'll tell you."

"There is a small fortune here," Cameron said.

"Not so small at all," Bowen said, grinning.

"So you're a rich man."

"Ye might say that."

"You were not poor in Scotland."

"Not in possessions," Bowen said. "Shall we take the air?" He put the chest back in place and covered the opening with loose stones.

Cameron stood with his back to the mine entrance and watched the crystal trickle of the little stream as it tumbled a hundred feet downward into the pool.

"A cooling dip?" Bowen asked. "There's no one to see."

"I want to go back to town," Cameron said.

"I had hoped for a wee bit of time with ye," Bowen said.

"You turn the Scot's accent on and off just as you do the false charm with which you've intrigued Cara," Cameron said.

"Ah. Don't be hard on me, boy."

"I? Far be it for me. You are a man grown and then some," Cameron said. "You left us of your free will, just as I, with my own free will, intend to return to Scotland as fast as I can. You'll not lack, for you have your gold, and I hope it can buy some contentment for you."

"I appreciate that sentiment," Bowen said, "but now I know, Cameron, that I would like to know you—and your sister. I had hoped someday . . ." He paused.

"As I said, you left us of your free will. What you did to mother . . ."

Bowen's voice was still soft, but there was a hint of steel in it. "Ye know not what I did to the woman, nor, apparently, what she did to me. That was none of your affair, after all."

There was a small voice inside Cameron telling him that he knew only one side of the tale, his mother's, and there was, for a moment, a desire to know more, but he turned and walked back toward the adobe hut and the horses.

That night there was a strange face in the cantina. Strangers were rare, but not beyond probability in Dos Caballos. Ordinary drifters didn't detour into the mountains. The man didn't look like a prospector or a hunter. Usually Catalina would have done her best to find out about the stranger, but she had eyes only for Cameron, who, at Cara's insistence, was seated with his sister at a table in the rear. His forehead was beaded with sweat, for the buxom Spanish matron in the kitchen had gathered a fresh batch of Mexican chile peppers and the bean-and-meat stew she'd made was quite fiery.

"Oh, Señor Lockhart," Catalina crooned, seeing that Cameron was having to wash down each bite with a gulp of Osa's home brew, "if it is too hot for you, I can have cook make a milder batch."

"No, no," Cameron said, gasping, "it's quite good. Very, ah, spicy."

"Make a man out of you," Mack Clemmons yelled from the next table. "Chili ain't worth eating unless it takes two bandannas to mop your forehead."

Lucky was at the bar. His eyes followed Catalina's every move and he couldn't help but note that she managed to pass by the Lockharts' table no matter which table she was serving. Once he glanced at Cara Lockhart, and she caught his eye and smiled. He lifted his glass in salute. Cameron motioned to him, patted an empty chair beside him. Lucky strolled over, loose-jointed and a little shy because Cara kept looking into his face and smiling.

"Mr. Smith," Cameron said, "we are interested in getting back to Socorro as quickly as possible."

"Too bad," Lucky said. "I know Bowen is enjoying your visit."

"When will you be making another trip?" Cameron asked.

Lucky looked around. The stranger was at the table in the corner, not far from the Lockharts' table, his hat low over his face, toying with a half-empty glass of Osa's beer. "Well, we don't have a set schedule yet. I was going to have a talk with my partner about that tonight."

"We're quite anxious," Cameron said. "Are we not, Cara?"

"Perhaps about different things," Cara said, causing Cameron to frown.

"Where is Bowen, by the way?" Lucky asked.

"He wanted to change," Cara said. "He'll be along."

"Well," Lucky said, rising, "I'll talk to Osa and let you know."

"Must you leave us?" Cara asked.

"Well," Lucky said, blushing, "I have to talk to Osa."

"I want to know what happened today between you and father," Cara said when they were alone. "Did you have words?"

"Very few," Cameron said.

"I don't understand why you're in such a dither to leave. A few days here won't harm us," she said.

Cameron had been doing a lot of thinking. He'd had time to remember all the old resentments. Logically he knew that it was problems between his mother and Bowen that had caused Bowen to disappear, but he'd been just a boy, and it had been natural for him to think that he, himself, had done something wrong, something terrible to make his father desert them. He was a man now, and he knew that he'd been blameless, but there was, deep inside, still the old hurt. He had told himself that regardless of what was wrong, he'd never desert any children of his.

"Do ye know why he so readily signed over the properties to me?" he asked, a hint of bitterness in his voice. "Because he's found gold. He's to be a very rich man. Our poor holdings in old Scotland would be small potatoes to a man with a chest of pure gold so heavy that it would take two strong men to lift it."

At the table behind them, the stranger's hand had been slowly turning his beer glass. His hands became suddenly motionless, and he looked up quickly from under his hat brim.

"I'm pleased for him," Cara said defiantly. "I am not ready to go, Cameron. If you insist on going, I will ask my father if I can stay for a few weeks. I'm sure he'll see me safely back to a place where I can take ship for Scotland."

"You'll do no such thing. You're only seventeen, Cara. I am your legal guardian. You will do as I say."

Cara was forming a heated reply when Bowen appeared, clean in his buckskins, tall, thick-chested. She forgot her anger and watched him walk toward the table. To that date, the men in her life had been gentlemen of the Tartan, and one, her paternal grandfather, now dead, had been a man much like Bowen, strong, assured. The others, on her mother's side, were, she now suspected, the kind of men that her mother had tried to make of Bowen, content to mind their holdings and say "Yes, dear." The combination of Bowen's Scot's manliness and the way he'd adapted to the American frontier and, according to Cameron, conquered it, made her quite proud to be the daughter of such a man. He was at home with the rather rough-cut denizens of this odd little town, and yet he still carried that gentlemanly Old World sophistication. And perhaps most importantly, when it came to her growing admiration for Bowen, there was, when he looked at her, such a warmth, such a love flowing from his eyes that it made her want to weep for pleasure.

She got in one more statement before Bowen reached the table. "I am going to spend some time with my father, with or without you, Cameron Lockhart."

Craw Maddock was doing something in which he took no pleasure. He was dozing, his head on his saddle, in a dry camp two miles out of Dos Caballos. When he heard the slow approach of a shod horse, he jerked into alertness and was ready, .44 in hand, when the horseman whistled and then approached the small fire. When the rider was near enough to be recognized, Craw holstered his pistol and answered the whistle. The rider went to the fire and poured coffee into a tin cup.

"You're back quick enough," Craw said.

"I seen all they was to see," the man said. His name was Little Ed Watts. He was just over five feet tall, skinny, and his face had the general outlines of a rodent. He was a drifter who was sometimes on Chunk Wilson's payroll. Craw had brought him with him into the Fray Cristobals because Craw was a cautious man who liked a whole, unperforated hide. He was careful enough not to go riding into Dos Caballos himself, since at least two men up there, the bastard who had coldcocked him and Lucky Smith, would recognize him.

"You gonna get around to telling me what you seen, or are you waiting for a band to put it to music?" Craw asked.

"They keep the coach in the stable," Little Ed said. "A man could come at it through the horse corral. One lantern kicked over and Mr. Wilson's ain't got no stage running competition on him."

Craw didn't think there'd be much to worry about in such an operation. "You see that Smith fellow?"

"They was all in the cantina," Little Ed said. "The big Mex, Smith, and your pal, the Scotsman. There with a pretty little piece, his daughter, and a dude son. Nothin' to worry about there."

"Take a lot to make me worry," Craw said.

"I had me a talk with a storekeeper's wife, big, loudmouthed woman," Little Ed said. "I didn't ask enough questions to make her leery, but I gather she don't really know—nobody does—where this Lockhart feller lives. Somewhere north, up in the mountains."

"He spends a lot of time in the cantina?"

" 'Bout the only place to spend time. That Mex makes a good bowl of chili."

"Well, I'm damned glad to hear you filled your gut," Craw said. He lay down. "Hear when they're going to run the coach down to Socorro again?"

"Heard 'em talkin' about it. The pretty little piece don't want to go. The brother is hot to trot. I'd guess soon." Little Ed poured out the grounds in the bottom of his cup. "We gonna take a stage on the roads, we need more men."

"I could take it by myself," Craw said. "Shut up and let me think."

A pack of coyotes were serenading from the top of a ridge. A hunting owl swooped low over the flickering fire.

"Craw?"

"I said shut up."

"They's somethin' else."

"All right."

"I heard that dude son tell his sister," Little Ed said, "that Old Lockhart's struck something up in them hills."

"So?" Craw asked.

"They was talkin' at the very next table. The boy said he knowed why the old man did something, I didn't get what, because he had a chest full of gold, enough to make him rich."

Craw sat up, his heart beginning to pound.

"Craw, we play our cards right, maybe we get something out of this 'sides a salary from Mr. Wilson," Little Ed said.

"Tell me what the dude said," Craw whispered. "Remember every word."

Craw knew the Fray Cristobals. Coming out of Texas with a posse hot on his heels, he'd lost himself there, almost starved until he got the hang of killing his own meat and discovered a Mex sheepherder's digs where he could buy beans and salt. He'd spent a lot of time up there with that Mex sheepherder, and the old man had shown him places where a man could hide out for years, if he had to, something nice to know for a man in Craw's line of work. He lay there looking up at the stars and pictured that country north of Dos Caballos in his mind. There were a couple of old Spanish roads that went nowhere and the creek that ran past Dos Caballos. For miles there wasn't anything else, except two little creeks that joined the larger one. To get north, a man had to take one of the old roads or ride along the stream.

He figured he could lie low up there until Bowen Lockhart started home and then follow him. He knew that he could spend half a lifetime up there looking for a shack, or a mine, or a panning site, and not find anything, but the man would have to go back to his gold sooner or later, probably after his son and daughter went back down the hill. He made up his mind that Chunk Wilson was going to have to wait a while before the Dos Caballos Stagecoach Company was put out of business by destruction of its rolling stock. With a chest of gold he wouldn't have to take orders from men like Chunk Wilson anymore. He'd heard that a man with money could live one fine life in San Francisco.

He took Little Ed through the whole story again next morning while Little Ed made the coffee and broke out hardtack and jerky for breakfast. Then he told the little man they were going back into Socorro to report to Mr. Wilson. He rode in front and kept looking for the right place. He found it when the old Spanish road corkscrewed up the side of a canyon. There was a drop of about a hundred feet into rock and brush, big enough to hide any army. He turned in his saddle and shot in the same motion. The .44 slug took Little Ed's horse right between the eyes. His second shot missed the spot he'd aimed at, right between Little Ed's eyes, but took off the top of Little Ed's head as if he'd been scalped. He was off his horse and giving one last kick to the jerking, dying horse in a flash, and the animal, with Little Ed's feet still in the stirrups, went crashing down. He stood there a while until the dust settled. The horse and man had been swallowed up by the brush. The coyotes and the buzzards would take care of the rest. He turned his horse, circled Dos Caballos to the west, and found a nice place to camp up north of town where he could see anyone coming or going toward his chest of gold.

Chapter Nine

Lucky was awakened just after sunrise by someone knocking on the big doors down below. He stuck his head out the hayloft door, brushing the straw out of his hair to look down on the carefully wrought magic of a feminine hairdo.

"Good morning, Mr. Smith," Cara said, beaming up at him.

Lucky jerked back. He was not exactly dressed for polite company, having slept in a pair of long johns cut off above the knees and at the shoulders.

"Mr. Smith," Cara called. He put just his head out. "Would you possibly have a horse I could hire?"

"No," Lucky said.

"Oh, please, I do want to see some of this wonderful country."

"Miss Lockhart, give me a minute," Lucky said.

He dressed in haste, went down with his hair still showing a bit or two of straw, and opened the big doors. Cara was as fresh as the morning in a fancy outfit obviously designed for riding sidesaddle.

"Miss Lockhart, all's I got is a jugheaded old horse and a mule, and the only saddles, well . . ." He motioned toward her quite stylish outfit. "What I mean is, well . . ."

"You don't have a ladies' saddle?" she asked, that smile of hers making Lucky's eyes blink.

"No, ma'am."

"I'm disappointed." She jutted out her chin. "Well, in that case, you do have a horse and a Western saddle, am I correct?"

"Well, yes."

"Please saddle the horse, then, and I'll be back within ten minutes."

"Have you talked to your father or your brother about this?" Lucky asked.

"Just have the horse ready, please," Cara said.

She was back in seven minutes by Lucky's old two-dollar watch. She wore a pair of her brother's riding breeches and a lacy man's shirt that showed her breasts to an advantage that made Lucky's eyes blink even faster.

"Miss Lockhart, I can't allow you to go off riding alone," Lucky said, looking at the ground, at the sky, anywhere but at those very obvious breasts and the way her hips filled out her brother's breeches.

"Then perhaps you can come with me?"

Lucky gulped. Old Jughead didn't have the energy to be dangerous, even for a woman. He had the mule. Coaly didn't take too kindly to the saddle, but he would do in a pinch with just a saddle blanket. "All right, Miss Lockhart," he said.

Coaly fought the bit and tossed his head and tried to kick something about ten feet behind him in thin air as they rode out of the stable. Cara sat the saddle well. Old Jughead was being a gentleman. Coaly settled down after a while, and Lucky took an easy path up the slope so that they could look back and see the view: Dos Caballos sort of fading in its adobe tans into the landscape, the little creek with its strip of green.

"It's so lovely, this country of yours," Cara said. "It seems to go on forever. One could just start out and ride and ride and never see a city or a house or another human being."

"Maybe a few Apache," Lucky said. "And you'd want to have some grub and know where there was water."

"It's the feeling of being so free," Cara said. "And there's a stark grandeur about it. Don't you just love living here?"

Lucky was struck dumb for a moment. "Well, I don't guess I ever really thought about it that way, not exactly."

76

"If I were a man, I'd seek out a land like this," Cara said. "And I'd carve myself a holding out of it and make it my own."

"Well, I reckon you could have about as much of this land as you'd want," Lucky said. "Ain't good for much. Sheepmen say that to get a flock across it they have to feed the sheep their own wool."

Cara laughed. "Are you, as we say out West, funning me, Mr. Smith?"

Lucky grinned. "Maybe just a little."

"Let's see what's beyond that ridge," she said, kicking gently at old Jughead's ribs. Coaly had recovered from his initial indignation and was following Jughead with his head down. Lucky could see the shape of the spreading hips of the girl ahead of him. He knew she was young, but girls married younger than she, and he wondered why some man hadn't climbed whatever mountain was necessary to have that girl. He was not thinking in personal terms, just admiring the view as he would admire a particularly colorful sunset or a field of cactus in bloom after a rain. Without even expressing it in thought, he knew that the likes of her, a foreign lady, was not for the likes of him. Hell, Osa didn't even think he was good enough for Catalina, a Dos Caballos girl.

Cara reined Jughead in on top of a barren ridge and looked out across a lonesome landscape toward the next rise of hills. "Yes, it is rather beautiful," she said.

After a few moments of silence Lucky said, "How is it back in Scotland?"

"Utterly boring," she said. "Rain, and tea at four, and stuffy old relatives and neighbors, and sheep that are such fragile creatures that they can find hundreds of ways of killing themselves."

"I know about sheep," Lucky said.

The way she said it didn't jar Lucky at all. "Yes, I have heard about your misfortunes." She smiled at him. "It was a terrible thing about your wife and son."

"Well, I've heard it said that the Good Lord won't put anything on us we haven't got the strength to stand, but there were times when I had my doubts." He had surprised himself. His remark to the young girl marked the first time he'd been able to say anything to anyone about the death of Maddy and the boy.

"But you don't give up, do you, Mr. Smith? You're trying now to make something of yourself with the stage line."

Lucky looked away. He wasn't used to being talked about in favorable terms. "There's a right pretty little valley not far off. Might see a deer or two there."

"I'd like that," she said.

For a time they rode side by side, and she talked about her life in Scotland, then asked Lucky questions about her father. Lucky told her about Bowen's celebration of the Queen's birthday, and she laughed merrily, throwing her head back to expose a trim throat so soft and pretty that it made Lucky *feel* lucky just to have seen her laugh so. They didn't see any deer. It was almost noon before they rode back into Dos Caballos to face a cold-eyed Bowen Lockhart and a furious Cameron.

"Just what in blazes were you thinking of, Smith," Cameron thundered, sounding just a bit like Bowen, "taking my sister off into the mountains alone?"

"I was thinking," Lucky said calmly, "that since she seemed to have a mind of her own and was determined to ride out that it would be better to have someone with her, even me, than for her to go alone."

"Cameron," Cara said, "please stop being an ass."

Bowen chuckled. "You must be hungry, girl," he said.

"I am famished," she said, leaping down from old Jughead to give her father a quick hug.

Now that Lucky had given proof that he could take the coach down the hill and back again, there was a sudden demand for transportation into Socorro. Lucky, not really realizing why, tried to put it off as long as possible. Mack and Zelma Clemmons had enjoyed their stay in the Socorro Hotel so much that Zelma, at least, wanted a repeat performance. Heck Logan had a small bag of dust he wanted to sell. Luke Malloy shocked the town by appearing in clothes with respectable patches and looking as if he'd either had a bath or fallen into the stream. With the demand there, Lucky had to give in. He told Bowen, who was staying temporarily in the boardinghouse to be near his children, that the stage would go next day. He was somewhat surprised when Bowen said that Cara and Cameron would be staying on in Dos Caballos for a while.

Lucky got the coach under way with an expert shot of the whip just over the leaders' ears. Heck Logan was up top with him; Mack, Zelma, and Luke inside the coach. Once again Osa had put his foot down and refused Catalina's tearful begging that she be allowed to go along, so the coach was not carrying at capacity. However, the availability of mail service had put almost twenty letters into Lucky's mail pouch.

It was Lucky's intention to duplicate the first trip, to reach the Rio Grande before stopping to make camp. He dreamed idly of having a change station between Dos Caballos and Socorro so that the trip could be made without stopping. He grinned at himself, thinking that he must be catching Osa's civic pride, imagining Dos Caballos to be something it might never be: a town of importance with enough people to make real stage service profitable. And then he tried to think of Catalina but saw, instead, Cara's face, sweet sympathy displayed on it as she spoke of the death of his wife and son.

Inside the coach, Zelma had started the men singing. The three voices were not concert quality, but it made for a rather cheery atmosphere as the stage rolled on at a good walk. Lucky took the coach up and down the switchbacks, over and down the hills, into the sweet little valley where once before the Chiricahua had stopped him. He had not given much thought to Nana and his spirit man's cravings for the shining wickiup on wheels, but once reminded, he looked around and saw only the shimmer of heat over the quiet landscape. He was totally surprised when an arrow thunked into the seat, brushing his leg before burying itself partially in the wood.

About twenty Chiricahua warriors came hooting and hollering out of the brush. If Lucky hadn't seen it, he wouldn't have believed it, even knowing that the Apache were probably the most skilled in conceal-ment. First it was quiet and peaceful, and those inside the coach were singing happily, and then the air was filled with Apache war cries and flying arrows.

Lucky spotted Nana, garish with war paint, leaning low over the neck of his horse as the Chiricahua rushed by the coach, loosing arrows. The first thing Lucky thought was how he admired the skill of those young riders, not a saddle among them. He recognized several of the warriors. Nana's band was made up of the youngbloods of the tribe, some of them, Lucky guessed, not over thirteen or fourteen. But he quickly came to understand that a barbed arrow fired by a strong thirteen-year-old can penetrate tender flesh as quickly as an arrow fired by a mature warrior.

"Nana," he yelled at the top of his voice, "now you cut that out."

He heard an explosion near his ear. Heck Logan was firing away with an old percussion pistol.

"Nana, someone's gonna get hurt," Lucky yelled as the young warrior came whooping back down on the other side of the coach.

Mack leveled his rifle out the window.

"Don't shoot the boys," Zelma yelled at him. "Shoot at the horses."

Mack's first blast knocked a young Chiricahua from the saddle, sending him tumbling into the dust. The horse whinnied in terror, bucked, and went racing off, eyes walled and mane streaming.

"Dammit," Mack said. "This thing always did shoot high."

Another Chiricahua yelped out in pain. Four guns were firing from the coach now, two rifles from inside, two pistols from atop. The Apache who'd been hit was streaming blood from his upper arm. Lucky dropped a horse and sent its rider tumbling. An arrow zipped by Lucky's cheek and he lifted a hand quickly. His fingers came away bloody.

"Nana," he yelped, "this is no joke, dadgummit."

Heck Logan burst out in a stream of the most fiery profanity Lucky had heard in a long time. He glanced over and saw an arrow buried into Heck's thigh. He dropped another horse and thought from the way the Apache fell that he might have broken his neck.

This time the Apache rode out of gunfire range and grouped around Nana.

"Lucky," Heck said, face pale, one hand pressing around the shaft of the arrow in his thigh, "we jest might have to start getting serious about this."

"We just might," Lucky said.

Zelma stuck her head out the window. "What are they doing?"

"I'm afraid they're trying to get up their nerve," Lucky said.

"I'm ashamed of that boy," Zelma said, "fighting like a Comanche instead of an Apache."

"If I was gonna be ashamed of him, I'd be ashamed of him for fighting his friends a-tall," Mack said.

"That boy used to hang around my store," Zelma said.

"*Our* store," Mack said.

"All eyes and belly," Zelma went on. "Loved horehound candy better'n snuff."

"Throw 'em a piece or two now," Luke Malloy said, "and maybe they'll ride on off."

"Here they come, Lucky," Heck said.

Nana was leading again. They were all in a line, bows ready, riding like the wind and whooping like a thunderstorm.

"Reckon we better not drop Nana," Lucky said. "That old chief wouldn't take kindly to that."

"It's *his* spirit man wants this coach," Heck said, "but I reckon you're right."

"Hold your dern fire," Zelma yelled, leaping out of the coach and running to stand about fifty feet from the coach, directly in the path of the charging file of Apache. She started waving her hands and yelling, "Nana, now you stop, you hear?"

It looked as if they were going to ride her down. She held her ground, yelling and waving her arms. The men on and in the coach held their fire. Nana jerked his horse to a dust-raising halt, the horse's muzzle inches from Zelma's face. She wiped horse spittle off her cheek and put her hands on her hips and looked up at the young man who would, everyone suspected, be chief of the Chiricahua one day.

"Jest what in the name of Old Scratch hisself are you up to, Nana?" Zelma demanded. "Git down off that horse, I want to talk to you."

"Woman, go," Nana shouted, pointing away from the coach.

"I'll do no such thing," Zelma said. "You already got some of your boys hurt, and I ain't gonna stand by and see any of them get killed. I'm ashamed of you. I know your papa done taught you better than to fight like some idiot plains Indian, riding up and down giving target practice to men with guns."

Behind Nana, a young brave yelled defiantly.

"You hush," Zelma yelled. "I'm talking to Nana."

"You speak truth," Nana said, holding up a hand to silence the muted yelps and grumbling from behind him. "The Apache way is the way of the mountain cougar, to lie in wait and pounce."

"It sure ain't riding around yelping and howling like coyotes," Zelma said. "Now you send them wild-eyed young bucks off, and you come help me see to your wounded."

Nana's face showed indecision.

"Big White Mother," he said, using the name for her which he had learned as a toddler when his father, the chief, took him to the Clemmons store to trade, "my spirit man hungers for that shining wickiup on wheels."

"Yes, and I'd guess you could take it, if'n you want to lose maybe half your warriors and start a war. What I reckon is that the old chief would be just a little mad if'n he knew what you were doing. What do you reckon?"

"He would not know. I would hide the shining wickiup on wheels in the mountains."

"Then you'd planned to kill me too?"

"No, Big White Mother."

"Well, if you take this coach and kill my friends, you'll have to kill me, else I'll go to your daddy as quick as I can and tell him."

"Kill the white eyes," a young brave yelped.

"Is this the day of Nana's shame?" another asked.

Nana turned and said, "*Cochones,* be silent." He looked at Zelma, still standing defiantly with her hands on her hips.

"From this day forward I will fight my friends no more," Nana said.

"All right," Zelma said. "Get off that horse and come help me."

Lucky breathed a sigh. He divided his attentions between Nana and Zelma as they checked the fallen. Heck had carefully cut a round hole in his pant leg and was using a razor-sharp knife to slice his wound large enough to be able to remove the arrow without tearing more flesh.

"Good Lord, Heck, doesn't that hurt?" he asked.

"Well of course it does, you derned fool," Heck said, jerking the arrow out. He leaned back. Blood poured up, and he thrust a dirty bandanna against the hole. "This don't stop bleeding, you'll have to cauterize it."

Three of the warriors, older than the others, were still on their horses, sitting straight-backed and severe as Zelma bent over a fallen Apache and slapped his face lightly until he sat up with a quick howl.

"Them three there," Heck said, "are calling this Nana's shame. They're saying that it is something he will have to redeem when he is war chief."

"Maybe that'll be a long time," Lucky said. "The old chief is a tough old bird."

Zelma tore off a strip of petticoat and bandaged a bleeding arm. "Bullet went clean through," she said in Spanish. "You keep it clean and you'll be all right."

When the wounded were treated, Zelma led Nana over to the coach. Lucky had climbed down. "I want you to give the boy a ride," Zelma said.

Lucky sighed. "Tie your horse onto the rear, Nana, and you can ride as far as you like with us."

Nana's eyes sparkled. He tied the reins of his horse to the coach and clambered up on top, stood there with his bow over his shoulder and his arms crossed. Lucky, who was a man of great patience but who had seen his patience tried severely, yelled, "Hyah," cracked the whip, and started the coach with a jerk that sent Nana tumbling all the way down the sloping boot of the coach to land heavily in the dirt. Nana leapt to his feet, ran, caught the coach, and scampered back to the top. This time he sat down, holding on with both hands. The warriors, a couple of them riding double, paced the slow movement of the coach, eyes looking straight ahead.

Coming up out of the valley was pretty spectacular, one of the most precipitous stretches of the road. At times it seemed that the outer wheels hung directly over the precipice and one could look from atop the coach to the canyon floor a couple of hundred feet almost straight down. At the top of the ridge Nana said, "Stop."

Lucky pulled the horses to a halt and let them blow with his foot on the brake to keep the coach from rolling back. Nana jumped down, loosed his horse, leapt astride and, with a whoop, led his troop back down the road toward the valley.

"What do you think?" Heck asked. He'd been able to stop the bleeding.

"I'm hoping his spirit man's hunger was satisfied when that rear wheel slipped and almost went over the edge and sent them rocks tumbling down," Lucky said.

Because of Heck's leg, Lucky drove on through the night, stopping only long enough to have Zelma boil up some coffee. They rolled into Socorro while it was still early and delivered Heck to a doctor's office. Lucky gave the horses extra care and extra oats and went to find his lawyer. He had some information for Sykes. He found Sykes drinking his breakfast, already in the office portion of his small frame house.

"I can't say for sure," Lucky said, "but I've asked around up in Dos Caballos, and the old-timers say they remember once when a stage came up to town—maybe ten, twelve years ago, maybe not that long. Time doesn't mean much in Dos Caballos. They say it was not a Butterworth coach but was out of California, maybe from Jim Birch's Pioneer Stage Company."

"That's a lot of maybes," Sykes said, offering the bottle, which Lucky refused with a shake of his head. "I'll look into it, though. You got any idea why a California coach would be all the way out here?"

"Nope," Lucky said. "Maybe you could write to the Pioneer Stage Company out in California."

"That'll take time."

"I've got time," Lucky said.

"Yeah, but has Wilson got time?" the lawyer asked. "Son, why don't you give it up? How many passengers you bring in today?"

"Four."

"How many people live in Dos Caballos and the mountains around?"

"I don't know. Forty, no more."

"You see?" Sykes shrugged. "And you are not going to get rich on what the post office pays you. Take the thousand and go on back up into the mountains or take your share of the profit and buy yourself a little piece of land somewhere where it rains more than once or twice a year."

Lucky thought about Sykes's suggestion as he walked down to the general store to fill Osa's shopping list. Maybe Sykes was right. In all truth, he wasn't too wild about riling Chunk Wilson. Then he remembered how Cara Lockhart's face had looked, there on a ridge looking up and across the Fray Cristobals.

"Don't you give up, Mr. Smith," she'd said. "You're trying to make something of yourself with the stage line."

Chapter Ten

Orejas de Lobo, Nana's father and leader of one of the smaller Apache groups in New Mexico Territory, had survived longer than any other Apache known to the tribe and longer than most white men. He had not lived to be ninety summers, ruling as chief for seventy of those years, by being either overly cautious or overly reckless. Lobo had not come from one of the old families from which the Apache traditionally choose a chief. He'd earned the honor. The Apache, mostly footloose, free-spirited, had a way of rewarding a man of ability. If a man happened not to be born to a special family that traditionally produced chiefs, and if he proved himself to be brave, resourceful, and worthy of leadership, others began first to associate with him and then to follow him. Thus Lobo, as he was most often called, began to gather young men to him when he was a boy of Nana's age, and thus he became the head of a shifting, varying, loosely knit "tribe" that, as time went on and Lobo became richer in years and wisdom, roamed from the rich hunting grounds west of the Rio Grande through the Fray Cristobals.

Lobo had seen many changes. He had won his reputation as a brave warrior against the Spanish. Although the Spanish had not been land-hungry, like the Anglos who followed them as self-styled "owners" of the ancient Apache lands, they had, at times, operated with a heavy hand, and it was honorable to chastise a few of them now and then. Their horses were fine animals and their women were moderately interesting, at least to the point where many a captured señorita had, in time, become a member of the tribe as the wife of a deserving warrior and the eventual mother of more warriors.

By the time the United States Congress made New Mexico a territory of the United States, Lobo was an old and much honored man. At first things had changed little. It didn't matter much to Lobo's people who sat in the governor's house in Santa Fe. Few Anglos ventured into the home grounds of Lobo's tribe. Life went on much as it had gone on before, with some of the women even planting corn, squash, and beans, for Lobo, as he grew older, came to like his comfort, and his wickiup had been in the same location for so long that the young men who now followed Nana couldn't remember when last the wolf's ears pointed toward a new adventure.

This life, which some thought too much like the life of other, less worthy peoples, the Navajo, for example, caused some of the younger warriors to question Lobo's leadership. Nana, however, would not hear a hint of criticism of his father. Although the old chief had several daughters, he had only the one living son, and that son was fiercely loyal, as well he might be, for no Apache had ever been more loved by his father.

Although he was still a boy, Nana had become, in the same way his father had become, a chief. He was called the War Chief by some, although there was no war with other tribes or with the Anglos. There were the occasional raids into Mexico, but the way was long and dry and hard, and not even the youngbloods wanted to undertake the journey too often.

Nana and those mostly young warriors who followed him were mobile enough to keep alive some of the traditions of the Apache, such as the ability to live off the land with wild, edible seeds and plants and meat from hunting. Nana's traveling group could break camp and disappear in a matter of minutes, could throw up a dwelling of branches and grass over a framework of poles in an hour. Nana and his young warriors were as hardy as hard living could make men, were expert observers of nature, masters of stealth and concealment, and for it all, many of them were still children at heart. Some understood Nana's preoccupation with the shining wickiup on wheels, for they, themselves, still could become enrapt with some childlike fancy.

On the other hand, Orejas de Lobo had a bit of difficulty even in realizing that Nana's brooding, his uncharacteristic edginess, came from an unfulfilled longing to own Lucky Smith's stagecoach for himself.

Concerned, Lobo suggested in his mild, wise way that perhaps it was time for Nana to lead another raid into Mexico, take a few horses and a couple of women, for nothing delighted an Apache's heart more than a new horse or a new woman.

"Go, my son," Lobo said. "Show your bravery once more, not that it is necessary, for it has been well established. Bring to me sleek, fat horses and take for yourself a pleasantly fat señorita and get sons on her, for it is time."

When not even those fine suggestions roused Nana from his malaise, Lobo began to be more concerned and inquired from some of Nana's followers the cause of his son's lack of interest in the finer things of life. One of the older warriors, feeling secretly that Nana's obsession with the stagecoach was not worthy, that it would be far finer to follow the old chief's suggestion to make another raid for booty into Mexico, told Lobo about the shining wickiup on wheels.

"Ah," Lobo said. He called his son to him and said, "We will go to the Anglo town."

Nana's face brightened. He was still smarting with shame over his failure to take the coach, over halting a war for one old, chubby Anglo woman. He gave a whoop and said, "I will tell the warriors to paint for war."

Lobo held up a hand. "There will be no war."

"Then why do we go?" Nana asked.

"We will talk with the Anglos."

"Talk?" asked a warrior when Nana told him that they would march with Orejas de Lobo at their head. "Talk is nothing more than quail feathers blowing in the wind." The warrior did not say as much to Nana, knowing Nana's loyalty to his father, but to others he said, "Lobo is old. He loves too much the coffee with sugar that he buys from the Anglo woman in Dos Caballos. We march not to war but to buy the follies of luxury for the old chief."

Whatever Lobo's reasons, it was an unusual event to see the old man preparing to march. The women and children were to be left behind, indicating that Lobo planned to return to his comfortable wickiup.

It was not a long march, except perhaps for a ninety-year-old who, even though he had chosen a fat and tame horse, felt each step of the horse throughout his old, weary bones. While Nana and his fast-moving young men ranged ahead and to the flanks, taking game, occasionally playing games of chase to pass the time required for the slow-moving main party to catch up, Lobo plodded along on his fat horse, stopping often to sit under a canvas sunshade to rest. Nana's spirit man grew impatient and filled the boy's heart and eyes with visions of the shining wickiup on wheels.

For a while Lucky had been a hero. The encounter with Nana had been told mainly by the men who were on the coach, and in that fine old tradition of the West, the accounts were far from conservative. Lucky, when telling both Catalina and Cara about the short-lived war while sitting at a table in the Dos Caballos, dwelt more on Zelma's part in ending the affair, but the other men were a bit more reluctant to admit that what had been a potentially disastrous situation had been defused by a mere woman. In the telling, somehow, Lucky's dead-eye accuracy with his old Colt became somewhat legendary, until the young sons of some of the Spanish families began to follow Lucky around, begging him to demonstrate.

Gradually, over a period of some forty-eight hours, Lucky's own version of the story began to prevail and he was no longer a hero, not even to the small Spanish boys. Zelma sat on the porch of the general store and maintained that she hadn't been about to let a bunch of good Apache kids get killed, not as long as she was ambulatory and had her tongue in her head.

"But you were quite brave," Cara had said when Lucky had tried, there in the cantina, to give all the credit to Zelma. "And I think it was very humane of you to shoot only at the horses, although I admit I hate to think of a horse being hurt, but better a horse than a man, instead of the Apache boys."

"Well, I don't *think* I hit any of the boys," Lucky said.

"I'm sure you didn't," Cara had said. She'd been leaning her chin on an elbow-propped hand, staring up into Lucky's eyes in a way that made his skin run with little prickles of pleasure.

Since Cara insisted on her daily ride, and Bowen spent a good portion of the day in the cantina, and Cameron seemed to be sulking, staying mostly in his room at the boardinghouse, it fell to Lucky to escort Cara. Once they headed northward up the stream to a little cascade over rocks that formed deliciously cool wading pools. There she told him to turn his head while she removed high-topped shoes and hose. When he looked back, hearing her delighted laughter, she was wading in ankle-deep water, with her brother's riding pants pushed up past her calves. Her skin was as white and unblemished as the first snow of winter, and Lucky turned his eyes away quickly to watch a buzzard come floating down to investigate the movement, hoping, buzzardlike, for the worst.

"Won't you join me?" Cara called. "It feels so good."

He pulled off his boots, his back turned toward her so that she wouldn't see the holes in the toes of his socks. The water did feel good. They walked, Lucky behind, up to the lower level of the multilevel drop, each shelf of rock in the falls not more than a foot or so high, and nothing would do Cara but to climb the steplike falls. He stayed close, and sure enough, he was needed when her bare foot slipped on a mossy rock and she tumbled backward, directly into his arms.

As he caught her, his hands closed over the soft flatness of her stomach and for a moment he felt girl sweetness under his palms before she had both feet under her and said, "Oh, thank you." She turned to face him and he guessed it was the sudden fright of the near fall that made her peaches-and-cream face a bit warm with a flush.

Of course, Cara spent a lot of time with her father, and rode with him as well. He told her that his home was too far north to make an easy ride for her, and she was not successful in convincing him otherwise. In the evenings she sat with Bowen, either on the boardinghouse porch or in the cantina. She knew just about the entire story of his travels now, how he'd tried buffalo hunting and was sickened by the slaughter and the waste, how he'd narrowly escaped having his scalp taken by a band of Comanche, how he'd sort of stumbled onto the idea of looking for gold in the Fray Cristobals while on the way toward California the hard way, across the deserts of New Mexico and Arizona.

Bowen did not mention his stash of gold to Cara. If he'd been asked, he would have said he assumed that Cameron had told her which, indeed, had happened. Cara, on her part, would have said that she felt it was Bowen's prerogative to talk about his gold or not talk about it. His having or not having riches didn't matter to her. He was her father and she had found that it was easy to revive the love she'd felt for him when she was a small girl.

One evening, after three pleasant days, one of them the day she waded in the water with Lucky, she said to Bowen, "I suppose I'll have to give in to Cameron and leave soon."

"Aye, I suppose you must," Bowen said. "How I will miss you, girl."

"And I you," she said.

"Will you ever come back to Scotland?"

"And what would your mother's rather wild-blooded male relatives say to that?" he asked.

She laughed. "As a matter of fact, a couple of them have sworn to shoot you on sight."

"So you see," he said.

"Would that really stop you if you wanted to come back?"

"Any activity that involves being shot on sight requires some thought," Bowen said. "When I am hungry to lay these eyes on the face of my daughter—"

"What if I stayed here?" she asked, watching his face, lit by a full moon, to see his reaction. He turned to look at her.

"This is a wild and hard country," he said. "There is no four-o'clock tea. The winds howl in the winter, and the women who come into this land weather and grow old quickly. No. You are a flower of a more gentle land."

"Scotland? Gentle?" she asked, laughing.

"More so than this."

She was silent for a moment. "And what will you do with yourself?"

He shrugged. "Present company excepted, of course, I have discovered that I have a bent for solitude."

"Somehow I don't see you as a perpetual hermit. Were you hurt that badly, Father, that you want to avoid all human contact, especially contact with women?"

His face froze. "Ye are treading on tender ground."

"If I can't, who can?" she asked. "You're still a young and vital man."

"Ha," he said.

"We could go to, as you say, a more gentle land. Catalina speaks of San Francisco as if it were the promised garden itself."

"Aye, we could." He took her hands in his. "And how long would you be content, living with an old reprobate like me? How long before you tired of it and married the first dirt kicker who came along? No. At home, with your beauty, ye'll have the choice of all the young cocks, and then you'll have your own holdings, as Cameron has his, and your children will not grow wild, as do the children in this land, but will be proper Scottish ladies and gentlemen."

She said, half laughingly, half seriously, "Well, I can tell when I'm not wanted."

"Darling girl," he said, his voice suddenly choked, "never, never think that."

She decided that Cameron and his sulking and his desire to leave quickly could go to perdition. When Bowen suggested a nightcap at the cantina, she agreed but asked him to wait while she rooted Cameron out of his room. She found him reading, teased and prodded until he agreed to accompany them.

Business was slow in the cantina. Only Lucky was there, leaning on the bar, making his one beer last. Osa was polishing mineral-fogged glasses with a dirty cloth. Catalina was seated rather demurely at a table reading a month-old newspaper. She leapt to her feet, smiling.

"You at least have made one conquest in this new world," Cara whispered to her brother. She expected him to laugh or make some slighting remark. To her surprise he looked at her rather oddly and then turned his face back toward Catalina, who was motioning them toward the largest and best table.

Well, well, Cara thought. And it was at that moment that a plan began to form. Catalina, in her youthful innocence, had been totally unable to conceal her fascination for Cameron, making her admiration so transparent that on previous occasions in the cantina Cara had watched only Catalina, not observing her brother's reaction. Perhaps, she felt as she watched Cameron's eyes follow Catalina's swaying movement after they placed their orders—whiskey for Bowen, beer for Cameron, sarsaparilla for Cara—she'd been conditioned by her own snobbery. Cameron was, after all, a somewhat wealthy, if not recklessly rich, Scottish landowner. Catalina was the daughter of a pub keeper. Had she not been already a bit conditioned by the democratic outlook of these people on the American frontier, to whom a man—or a woman—was nothing more or nothing less than what he or she proved to be in living action, she could not even have imagined her brother being interested in a girl obviously so far below his class according to Old Country standards. Now, with her desire not to leave so quickly, anything seemed possible. Lady that she was, she did not for a second consider the possibility of Cameron's dishonoring this spritely little Spanish girl. When a lady thought of relationships between man and woman, she heard the soft clanging of wedding bells.

So, on a clean summer night, with only the three of them and Lucky Smith in the cantina, it did not seem too outlandish to imagine that Cameron's gaze toward Catalina indicated more than a man's appreciation for a fine form, in the same way that a man will follow the movements of a particularly fine horse. Cara had no idea, for her gentle and moral nature would not have allowed such a possibility, that she was to be instrumental in the ruination of Osa's daughter.

"Cameron," she said, "you've been an absolute bore. Here we are in a new country, with beautiful natural features, and you spend all your time either here or in the boardinghouse. Why don't you ride out tomorrow and see some of the landscape?"

She had started the question just as Catalina came swaying from the bar, tray laden with their refreshment. Catalina arrived as she uttered the last sentence.

"Yes, Señor Cameron," she said, "your sister is right. You should take a ride."

"Only if you'll be my guide," Cameron said, to his surprise as much as to the surprise and pleasure of Cara and Bowen.

Cameron was even more surprised when, with a smile that showed her white, perfect teeth, Catalina said, "Good. I will meet you just after sunup at the northern end of town beyond the stables."

When she was gone, Bowen grinned and said, "Cameron, I think that means she's going to sneak off from that old bear of a father of hers. Beware."

"Really, Father," Cameron said, "she's an adult, after all."

Bowen was silenced for a moment, wondering if Cameron realized that he'd called Bowen "Father" for the first time. "Don't take it lightly. Osa keeps a club, a very wicked shillelagh of a club, under the bar to protect his daughter's virtue."

"Come now." Cara laughed. "Cameron is a gentleman."

"So he is," Bowen said, "and speaking of gentlemen, let's not have Mr. Smith standing all alone at the bar. Any objections?"

"Of course not," Cara said, herself calling out Lucky's name and inviting him over.

Cameron almost did not go. He was up before light, stoked his inner man at the Widow Brown's breakfast table with a chunk of the previous night's leftover venison covered with the running yellows of four eggs; huge, white, fluffy biscuits dripping with freshly churned, sweet butter; and topped it off with more biscuits and butter covered with honey. He asked himself repeatedly what the Hades he thought he was doing, where did he think he was, who was this girl with whom he was meeting, and when would he assert his manhood and his legal guardianship of his sister to put her on board the coach and head down the mountains toward home? He was still asking variations of the questions of himself when he rode past Lucky's establishment and saw, on the road to the north, a vision in black.

Catalina wore a riding outfit that Osa had been saving for San Francisco, the traditional round crowned hat with a flat, beaded brim, the frilly white blouse and leather vest, the split skirt that came only to her knees, fine leather boots adorned with silver spurs, making for a composite, with Catalina's natural, slim, yet rounded beauty, that left Cameron quite breathless.

"We will ride quickly to the top of the hill and over it," Catalina said, mounting easily with a swing of leg that showed youthful grace.

So as not to be seen from the town, Cameron thought, kicking old Jughead into a reluctant lope to follow her spirited horse.

The inevitable happened on a mossy bank, with the sun warm on bare, sweetly scented, dusky, Spanish girl flesh. Years later, when she was a matron of position, Catalina would copy down in a neat, feminine hand in her journal three quotes from a man of whom she had never heard on that brilliant summer's day when she rode out with a young Scottish laird to show him the wonders of her country and lead him to the same tricky, step-falling cascade of the stream where Lucky and Cara had waded just two days previously. Not only did she not know the man's name whose explanations of her actions on that day would so ease her of a long-standing guilt, but she had never, on that day, attempted to read a book of the daunting thickness of the book from which she copied Leo Tolstoy's words of rationalization for her total, sudden, and quite unexpected fall from innocence.

"God would not have put into her heart an impulse that was against His will."

"It is not given to man to know what is right and what is wrong. Men always did and always will err, and in nothing more than in what they consider right and wrong."

"All will be forgiven her, for she loved much; and all will be forgiven him, for he enjoyed much."

Was it the same residue of childhood that tempted Catalina to take off her boots and hose and wade, holding her riding skirt to her knees? Was it the same mossy rock that caused her foot to slip and produce the same actions that had seen Cara fall back into Lucky's arms? Certainly the actions that followed Catalina's slip differed from those of Lucky and Cara. Cameron, feeling the lithe slimness, the heat, the softness in his arms, lost all common sense, found Catalina's lips, and she, previously unkissed, showed the same ability to learn quickly what would, in later years, make her quite the well-read lady.

It happened behind a curtain of privacy formed of miles of wilderness, a thinly populated area of mountains, and the brush and trees that formed a hedgelike barrier along the creek.

"My God, what have we done?" Cameron cried when it was over.

"There are many names for it," Catalina said, herself crying inside, *"Por Dios!"*

"I will speak with your father the moment we get back," Cameron said, overflowing with the residue of his experience and with honor.

"Loco, ca," she said. "Idiot."

"We will, of course, be married," he said. He was not without experience. He had been, after all, a Scottish laird, and the man of the house, since his twelfth birthday, and in spite of its unfavorable climate, its stark landscapes, Scotland was not left out of the world when the distribution of hot-blooded wenches was made. He was not a roué by any means, but he knew a virgin when he had one.

"*Una impossibilidad,*" she whispered.

"Why?"

"My father will have me marry a man of Spanish blood, a San Francisco gentleman."

"But—"

"If he even suspects," she said, "he will mash out your brains with his club."

"But—"

Catalina's mind was moving with the speed of a frightened roadrunner. She had not intended it to happen. It *had* happened, as if they were both under the influence of an *encantador*. She was damaged goods now, but she was not one to weep over a loss that at the moment she could not find the strength to regret. "I will tell you what," she said. "We will ride here again, tomorrow, and speak of this."

On the morrow it happened more deliberately, with more intense and curious mutual exploration, and the conversation following was more of the same.

"What would you do, stay?" she asked.

"No, I will have to go home."

"And I? What will your fine gentlemen and ladies say when you tell them you have brought a wife from a cantina in a two-horse town in the American West?"

"I don't care about that," he said.

"But I do," she said. "I will be a great lady in San Francisco. My father's dowry will see to it."

"Catalina—"

"We will ride out no more," she said, "for I do not want a child from this."

He flushed. He had just been as intimate with her as it is possible to be between man and woman, and yet her frank language shocked him.

"As you say," he said.

There was a bit of weeping into a pillow that night, but not out of regret. And yet it was not for lack of morals that she did not regret. She would never understand it, not for years, not until she had matured with age and had encountered the simple sophisms of Leo Tolstoy in *War and Peace*, how she could so willingly give herself to a man with whom she knew there was no future. At the time she merely told herself that she was in love with the most beautiful man she'd ever seen, and that her act was, in part, a rebellion against being merchandised in San Francisco with her father's dowry with the objective of buying a respectable husband, not because she wanted him but because her father wanted her to have a respectable Spanish husband and grandchildren of the blood for himself.

"I am ready to go to San Francisco," she told Osa that night.

"Soon, soon," he said.

Chapter Eleven

It was Osa, himself, who first saw the visitors. He had indulged a bit, drinking his own brew with some cowboys who had detoured into the cantina from the south, and his bladder sent him to the little house behind the cantina just as the summer sun was putting the first hint of crimson into a small band of sky above the eastern hills. They were nothing more than stationary shadows at first, and then, as he came out, letting the slab door slam behind him on its spring, he saw them more clearly.

He estimated that there were fifty of them, silent, motionless, horses almost as motionless as their riders, moving only to flick a tail or shift weight from one front leg to the other. They ranged up the little slope to the west, down toward the creek on the south, across the road to the north, and there were six or seven of them down the slope on the near bank of the creek.

Osa tugged at his trousers and thought about it. He thought he could recognize some of them as being friends of Nana, but he didn't see the young war chief himself. He raised a hand in greeting and went back inside to waken Catalina and to put on his shirt.

By the time he and Catalina came out onto the porch, others had seen the Apache surrounding the town and were beginning to gather in little clumps, one group of them moving toward the cantina, the other up toward the stable where Osa saw Lucky come out and look around in a three-hundred-sixty-degree circle.

Osa grunted and told Catalina to go tell matron to prepare breakfast. Others missed breakfast as they waited for the silent Apache to move, to whoop, to do something. A few guns appeared in the streets. When Osa and Catalina came back out, everyone in Dos Caballos was there. Still the Apache hadn't moved.

All three of the Lockharts had come out of the boardinghouse to stand with Lucky in front of the Clemmons General Store. Bowen had his dueling pistols in his belt and carried his Sharps.

"I hope you won't need those," Lucky said.

"I echo that sentiment," Bowen said.

"Marvelous," Cameron said. "Bloody marvelous."

"Don't sound like an effete Englisher," Cara said.

"Actually, they are magnificent," Cameron said. "How can they be so still for so long?"

"I don't care how. I want to know why," Bowen said.

"I think we'll know soon," Lucky said.

He'd heard a jingling sound from the road leading south along the creek. And then, to confirm his suspicions, several strong, guttural voices started singing an Apache song of greeting.

"Hell," Zelma said from the porch of the store, "it's a damned social call, that's all."

"Really marvelous," Cameron said when Nana and Orejas de Lobo turned onto the main street of Dos Caballos and came into full view. The boy seemed to loom larger than the sere and withered old man, but there was a straightness of back, a natural dignity in the ninety-year-old chief that pleased Cameron's eyes.

"By God, it's old Wolf's Ears himself," Zelma said. "This must be an occasion to get that old bastard off his sleeping skins."

Five young warriors rode behind the two chiefs, singing the song of friendship and greeting. The horses were walking, so that it took a long time for Lobo and Nana to reach the general store. Once there, the singing stopped.

"They know how to make an entrance," Cameron said.

"Hush," Zelma hissed.

"Big White Mother," Lobo said, "I greet you."

"It's good to see you, Orejas de Lobo," Zelma said. "Why don't you get down and set a spell."

"Is there coffee and sugar?" Lobo asked.

"Yes, sir, you bet," Zelma said. "Mack, get a chair for the chief."

"No chair," Lobo said, creaking down off his horse, toddling stiffly to sit on the edge of the porch. Zelda had a steaming tin cup of coffee in his hand within two minutes. Nana was sitting his horse stiffly, not deigning to look at the curious faces all around him. And all around the town the warriors sat—motionless, silent, menacing.

"Good, good," Lobo said after draining coffee so hot that it would have boiled potatoes and extending the cup for a refill from the pot Zelma had brought to the porch.

"He who makes the day has done well," Lobo said after quickly finishing the second cup and refusing the third with a horizontal wave of his hand.

"It's a nice one," Zelma said.

"We praise such a day in song," Lobo said.

"We do, too," Zelma said. "The Good Book says, 'This is a day the Lord has made, let us rejoice and be glad in it.' "

Lobo chuckled dryly. "So you have not yet given up on converting me to sing the praises of your god with three heads."

"Nope," Zelma said. "There's time yet. You're still a young man."

Lobo chuckled again. He looked around, pointed a stiffened finger at Lucky, and asked Zelma, "This is the man who drives the gleaming wickiup on wheels?"

"Uh-oh," Lucky said under his breath.

"In the flesh," Zelma said.

"I will speak with you," Lobo said.

Osa and Catalina had just arrived, having walked slowly from the cantina. Lobo lifted one hand. "Greetings, amigo," he said.

"You honor us with your presence, great chief," Osa said so smoothly and diplomatically that one of Lucky's eyebrows shot up in surprise.

"I have come to talk with the man who drives the shining wickiup on wheels," Lobo said. "To talk sense with him." There was, in the old chief's face, just a hint of the old fire, enough to make Lucky feel uneasy. Apparently Nana's spirit man had not been satisfied with a ride on the coach.

"Well, chief," Lucky said. "I will listen and try hard to use good sense."

"My son, Nana," Lobo said, waving a hand. Nana's frozen expression did not alter.

"Nana and I are acquainted," Lucky said.

"And you know that Nana's spirit man hungers for the shining wickiup on wheels."

"Well, chief," Lucky said, having just about decided that the dadgummed Apache were serious about it this time, that Nana had convinced his father that it was worth killing a few Anglos for the coach. As much as Lucky was attached to the coach, and as much as it pleased him to be half owner and to be somebody, he didn't see that it was worth dying for and taking most of the town, or all of it, with him.

"Great chief," Osa said before Lucky could tell Lobo to take the coach and live happily ever after with it, "there is this about the shining wickiup on wheels. I have invested much money in that coach."

"You?" Lobo asked.

Now Nana's face changed. His mouth drooped and there was a sullen squint to his eyes.

"Yes, great chief," Osa said. "It is I who have invested the money. This man is my partner, my amigo, who owns but half the coach and has invested only work, not money. It was I who bought the horses."

"You bought horses?" Lobo asked. "Why did you not ask me? We have horses."

"It takes specially trained horses, Orejas de Lobo, my friend," Osa said. "But I am grateful that you would think to let me have horses."

Lobo was silent. Nana was glowering. "Let me understand, my old friend," Lobo said. "You say you bought the horses. It is not the horses that my son's spirit man craves, but the coach."

"But when I put up the money, I bought half of everything," Osa said, "so that the coach, which, after all, is the heart of the thing, for without the coach there are only horses and women cannot ride up and down the mountains, and we cannot carry in the things we need without the coach, so that the coach is half mine as well."

Lobo gave a sign with his hand, indicating that the matter was closed.

100

Nana continued to glower. Lobo looked at Zelma and smiled, showing stubs of blackened teeth. "But then the trip is not totally wasted, Big White Mother, for I have a bit of Mexican gold to pay for coffee and sugar."

"Just name the amount," Zelma said.

Nana kicked his horse and whirled him, almost knocking down several people, and thundered down the street to the south. Zelma and Mack brought coffee and sugar, and it was duly loaded behind two of the warriors who had sung the song of greeting.

"You don't have to run off, Lobo," Zelma said. "Have another cup on me before you go."

"He who makes the day will be finished with his work before I have reached my camp," Lobo said. He rose, tottered a bit, clutched at his chest, his face contorted. Zelma leapt to catch him before he fell. She held him there. He began, in a weak, tinny voice, to chant the Apache song of death.

"Someone better get Nana back here quick," Zelma said. "I think it's his heart."

Osa spoke in the Chiricahua language to a warrior. The young man raced his horse away and was back, with Lobo lying on a blanket on the porch, chanting the death song feebly. Nana knelt by his side and the old man looked up.

"They have poisoned you," Nana said.

"No such thing," Zelma said. "Look." She poured coffee from the pot and drank.

"No poison," Lobo croaked. "Now you are chief, my son. Remember that the vows of your father and your father's father hold you."

After a long time Zelma put a hand on Nana's shoulder. "He's gone," she said.

With a power that rasped his throat, Nana started screaming the death song, and the other warriors joined in, with voices coming now from the warriors who surrounded the town.

"Nana," Zelma said, "you can use our wagon to take him home."

"No wagon," Nana said.

Nana gave orders. Two young warriors raced toward the creek, where there were some green saplings growing, and returned in a few minutes with cut poles. Only a few of the warriors had joined the group in front of the store. The majority of them still sat motionless on their horses, surrounding the town, but the Apache death song was issuing from all throats, filling the entire town with the sound of mourning, echoing off the walls of the canyon.

Osa said, "Nana says that the great chief, his father, rode into this place, and that he will ride out."

Men tied the dead chief's feet together with a rope under his horse's belly, then braced him with the poles, lashed ingeniously to hold him in an upright position, one short stick thrust into his clothing to hold up his chin.

With a wail Nana bent, lifted dust from the street, and showered it over himself, rubbing it into his face. Then he took the reins of the dead chief's horse and started walking, the chant of the death song marking his paces.

Lucky took off his hat, and silently the other men of Dos Caballos followed his example.

When Nana and the small, attendant band reached the end of the street, past the cantina, the other warriors began to fall in behind. Soon the last of them had disappeared down the road to the south.

"How sad," Cara said. Lucky was touched to see that she had tears in her eyes.

"I think there'll be trouble," Mack said.

"Naw," Zelma said. "That boy knows me too well to think I'd poison an old friend."

The Widow Brown said, "You just can't trust Injuns. Shouldn't we send word up north, to Santa Fe, see if we can get some Army boys in here for protection?"

"Them boys is all busy fighting the Confederates come in from Texas," Mack said. "Not much chance of getting Army in here, even if we needed 'em."

"We won't need 'em," Zelma said. She looked directly at Osa. "Will we, Osa?"

"Perhaps not," Osa said.

"I think you know for sure," Zelma said. "I knowed for a long time there was something special between you and them Chiricahua. How come old Lobo was going to take the coach away from Lucky but not from you?"

"With the Apache, who can tell?" Osa said.

"I think we got a right to know," Zelma said.

"It is a long story and it goes far back in time," Osa said.

"I'd kinda like to hear that story," Lucky said.

"Another time." Osa grunted.

"Now, Osa," Zelma said, "Lobo said something about Nana remembering his vows. Would that have something to do with you?"

"It was a vow made between my father and Lobo," Osa said.

"Would, by any chance, that vow give protection to us, as well as to you?" Zelma asked.

Osa shrugged. "He who says he knows the heart of the Apache lies."

"That don't tell us much," Zelma said.

"No, it does not," Osa said, taking Catalina's arm and turning to walk back toward the cantina.

After a while Lucky walked down toward the cantina. The town looked normal again, although, no doubt, there were some lively discussions going on here and there as to the intentions of the Apache. Lucky had his one beer for the day, although it was still quite early. He waited until the cantina was empty.

"Osa," he said, "I'd like for you to tell me the answer to that question Zelma asked. Why would Lobo have been willing to take the stage from me and not from you?"

"It doesn't matter," Osa said. "Just know that they will not take the coach." He grinned. "They might kill you, but they won't take the coach."

"Because it's half yours?"

Osa sighed and looked around. Catalina, occupied with her own thoughts, had gone into the living quarters. "Have you never wondered why, in the history of this town, the Apache have harmed no one, taken no captives, stolen no loot?"

"Well, I thought, I guess, that it was because old Lobo liked to trade at the Clemmons store and because maybe he considered us to be friends."

"The Apache has no Anglo or Spanish friends, not unless there is blood involved," Osa said, "or something greater."

"Are you saying it's because of you?" Lucky said. "I know you've been here a long time."

"And my father and grandfather before me," Osa said. He sighed again. "All right. There is no harm in telling you this. When my grandfather was still alive and my father was a young boy, this land was still Spanish. The supply trains made a long, long trip up from Ciudad Juarez, in Mexico, and were often raided by the Apache. There was war all along the trail from Mexico to Sante Fe, and the Apache in this area were led by Lobo's father. To make the route safe, a large force of mounted lancers was sent, and one day they stumbled onto the Apache village by accident while Lobo's father and the warriors were away. My grandfather, who had been hunting, heard the firing and investigated. He saw the soldiers killing old men, women, and children, and he saw a two-year-old boy running from a mounted soldier armed with a drawn saber. He shot the soldier in ambush. He ran out of hiding, carrying the two-year-old boy with him. His killing of the soldier and his saving the boy were seen by a woman, the boy's mother, who lived with her terrible wounds long enough to tell Lobo's father that his son had been saved by the keeper of the Dos Caballos cantina, my grandfather."

"I'll be darned," Lucky said. "So your grandfather saved old Lobo's life when he was a boy. That's why the vows."

"Lobo's father vowed that as long as a Carranza wanted to live in Dos Caballos, he would be safe, he and all that was his." He shrugged. "Where would I be, where would my grandfather and my father have been without customers? So the whole town is safe from the Apache."

"Remind me not to give up drinking," Lucky said.

"My father and Lobo were friends as boys. They hunted together. As you know, Lobo later developed a taste for coffee with sugar and he would bring his son, Nana, into Dos Caballos to trade at the store, something he'd been doing before Nana was born, and before Mack and Zelda came to take over the store. My mother was a gift to my father from Lobo."

"I'll be," Lucky said. "But she wasn't Apache."

"Yes," Osa said.

"Well, then, I don't understand," Lucky said. "Because Catalina sure ain't half Apache."

"So you demand all of it?" Osa said.

"I don't want to be nosy, Osa, but since you're talking, I will admit to a mite of curiosity."

"So," Osa said, "we are business partners. You are younger than I, and we are friends. I have no one to care for Catalina if something should happen to me, if my heart should give out as Lobo's did. I will tell you. Catalina, too, was a gift. But to me, not to my father."

Lucky was wisely silent, because he could sense Osa's reluctance to go on.

"Now and again I would take my wife to visit her people in the Apache camps, to hunt and drink mezcal with my father's friend, Lobo, and with my wife's brothers. There were many raids in those days, when Lobo was young and hot-blooded, and there were nearly always Mexican women as captives. Then there was one, sick, large with child, the child thought to be of Lobo's seed. She died in birth and the child had no Apache features. When Lobo saw this, saw that the child was obviously not his but had been seeded before the woman was captured, he was angry and thought to kill the child. My wife, who was barren, begged to be allowed to save the girl child, to have it as her own."

"Catalina," Lucky breathed.

"Catalina," Osa said. "My wife died when Catalina was less than a year old."

"Well, Osa," Lucky said, not knowing what else to say. "You sure done a good job of raising her."

Osa's eyes gleamed with pride. "Yes, she is my one joy, my friend. There are times when I am overwhelmed with her, with this jewel, who is as dear to me as if she were the seed of my own loins. I stand in wonder that such a thing, such a thing of grace and beauty, could have come from a common *puta*."

Lucky swallowed.

"For the Apache took the woman from the brothel in Ascension," Osa said. "And this child, with an unknown father, is more my own than you can imagine, my friend, and will marry well, and give me beautiful grandchildren."

Lucky knew that Osa would not say more. He finished his beer. Neither of them were aware that Catalina had started back into the cantina, only to hear the last part of Osa's recital.

Stunned, she had stood behind the cloth drapes over the door, waiting for more, waiting to hear her father say that it was all a lie. And when he was silent, and Lucky went away and Osa leaned wearily over the bar, she walked, straight-backed, stiff-faced, to her room to lie on her bed, eyes staring at the ceiling. Now she knew why she had felt no guilt there on the mossy riverbank. Like mother, like daughter. What more could be expected of the bastard daughter of a common whore?

Chapter Twelve

Chunk Wilson rode one of his own stages south from Santa Fe with the growing knowledge that all business was not as simple as ranching. When the opportunity to buy certain portions of the old Overland Mail routes came, it seemed like a good idea at the time, but now, after running into obstacle after obstacle in his efforts to connect the El Paso to Santa Fe route with a through route to the west, either through Lordsburg and Tucson to Yuma and San Diego, or northward through Gallup and Flagstaff, he found himself longing for the old days when all he had to worry about was keeping a few cowboys and a few thousand longhorns reasonably content. He'd sold his holdings in the fine grasslands of the northeastern part of the territory, and now he had every penny he owned sunk into what was turning out to be a bottomless pit.

Hell, there were times nowadays when he longed for times even further in the past, when he had roamed with nothing more than a bedroll, a slicker, a handgun, and a rifle, taking opportunity where it came.

He was in a black mood when the coach rolled into Socorro. While washing the dust of the road from his mouth and throat at the Socorro Saloon, he looked around and saw a few strangers and a few familiar faces, many of whom were in his employ. He asked about Maddock and his usually warm eyes were hardened when he was told that no one had seen Craw for a few days. He asked casually if the coach from Dos Caballos had made another trip into Socorro and his eyes glinted when someone said that, no, his competition had not been into town of late.

Logically he knew that Lucky Smith's one coach was no threat to his plans, but he'd just come from meetings where men had tried to rob him just as surely as if they'd had a gun on him, and he was in no mood to be tolerant. The very fact that some people in Socorro thought it was funny to have a stage not owned by Wilson pulling into town at irregular intervals was enough to make Wilson think dark thoughts about what was going to happen to that coach and to its owner if he stood in the way.

He called one of his men over to the table he'd been occupying alone. "Where the hell is Maddock?"

"He pulled out of here about four, five days ago," the man said. "Had a bedroll and a spare horse. Didn't say where he was headed."

He had better damned well have been headed for Dos Caballos, Wilson was thinking. His eyes softened again. Maddock was a good man. He'd get the job done. He was probably waiting for Smith to start another run down the hill so that he could do the job away from witnesses.

Craw Maddock had spent three days and three nights camping, an activity that did not please him, in the hills north of Dos Caballos. Once he'd seen Bowen Lockhart ride out of town with his son, but the two men rode west, not north, and Maddock spent a good portion of a day trailing them, only to find out that they were hunting. He was getting damned impatient. He decided he was going to give it one more day and then he might just ride into Dos Caballos himself and see if he could raise a little dust.

On a typical summer's morning Cara walked to Lucky's stable, intent on riding again, only to find that Lucky had a job to do. A sheepherder had brought in two mules to be shod. Now that she knew the type of country around Dos Caballos, Cara was not stubborn enough to insist on riding alone, so she watched Lucky heat and pound metal into shape for a while, rather liking the way his forearms muscled up as he used the hammer, finding the ring of hammer on anvil to be a certain kind of rustic music.

Lucky had trouble keeping his mind on his work. At the risk of missing the red-hot shoe entirely with the hammer, he kept sneaking looks at Cara. She had her hair piled atop her head and secured there with mother-of-pearl combs. She looked as fresh as a mountain spring. When she left, walking back toward the boardinghouse, Lucky paused in his work and watched her go. He couldn't keep from dreaming a bit. It was pleasant, and it made his heart rate increase, and then he remembered. He was a sheepherder who had killed his own herd. He made just enough money in the stable and smithy to buy beans. He had as much business dreaming about a Scottish lady, who would be leaving soon to put thousands of miles of land and water between them, as a carrion crow had dreaming about a mockingbird.

Bowen and Cameron had ridden out again together. Although she was pleased to think that Cameron was, after all, getting to know his father a bit better and, it seemed to her, coming to like him a little, that left Cara at loose ends. She wiled away some time talking with Zelma at the store, then wandered down to the cantina. Osa was sitting at a table, the place empty, his feet up, eyes closed. He opened one eye when he heard Cara's footsteps and then came to his feet, bowing and smiling.

"What can I do for the lady?" he asked.

"Nothing, really," she said. "I was just—"

"There is a fresh pot of coffee," Osa said.

"Very well," she said, sighing and taking a chair. "That is very kind of you, Señor Carranza."

"May I sit with you?" Osa asked when he came from the kitchen with a mug of coffee.

"Please do," she said. "In fact, I've been wanting to speak with you. I am told that you have been here longer than anyone."

"Longer than God himself," Osa said.

Cara blushed at the near blasphemy. "I'd so like to hear about the early days, when the land was under the rule of the Spanish."

Next to selling something to drink or eat to anyone, Osa liked talking best. He launched into an account of how his grandfather had come into the mountains looking for gold and had stayed to make the best beer north of Mexico City. Cara was a good audience. She listened through another cup of coffee, and then the sheepherder whose mules Lucky was shoeing came in and Osa went to the bar to serve him. Cara was preparing to go back to the boardinghouse when Catalina came in, smiled weakly, and stood indecisively in the doorway. There was a slight puffiness around Catalina's huge, dark eyes. Cara sensed that all was not right, stood, called out Catalina's name, and asked her if she'd sit with her for a while.

Catalina saw what Cara was drinking, offered a refill. Cara already felt overly full but accepted. The talk, when Catalina came back, was small, with Catalina commenting on the way Cara had done her hair, on the ruffly top she wore with Cameron's riding pants. Catalina was wearing black silk, with lace and ruffles, the long, sleek Spanish look complementing her smooth, sultry complexion and her dark hair and eyes.

Cara remarked on the beauty and grace of the gown.

"This is nothing special," Catalina said.

"What do you mean nothing special?" Osa shouted from the bar. "It came all the way from Mexico City, and it was not cheap, mind you."

Catalina laughed.

"One cannot have a proper conversation about woman things with men listening," Cara said.

"Would you like to see the gowns that I am saving for San Francisco?" Catalina asked. Cara said she'd love to.

Catalina's room was neat, with heavy Spanish furnishings in glowing, dark wood. A huge wardrobe that Cara thought must have been a wagonload in itself held gowns in reds, blacks, and violets. Cara oohed and ahed, wondering how she would look as a Spanish señorita, an unlikely thought since her auburn hair, blue eyes, and delicate skin were quite un-Spanish. As if reading her thoughts, Catalina said, "Please try this one. I think you would be beautiful in it."

Cara protested only slightly. With the black, silky, lacy gown on, she whirled in front of Catalina's mirror and laughed. She had to admit it, she was just a little bit striking.

"You will stun them in San Francisco with this," Cara said.

She saw a shadow pass fleetingly over Catalina's face. "Catalina, is something wrong?" she asked.

"No, nothing." Catalina helped Cara out of the gown, hung it up, turned. "I will not know how to conduct myself in San Francisco," she said. She did not take time to analyze her sudden reservations about a plan that Osa had been talking about since she was ten years old. "Sure, I have the clothes, but there is more to being a lady than clothes."

"You are a natural lady," Cara said. "You have poise and you are quite charming."

Catalina turned away, wondering to herself if her mother, the *puta*, had also had charm. That knowledge was the reason she had come to dread the idea of having her father take her to San Francisco, into polite society. She was the daughter of a *puta*. She was a country girl. She could attract all male eyes in the Dos Caballos Cantina and, until Cameron Lockhart had come along, handle any man; then her heredity surfaced in her conduct with Cameron.

"Thank you," she said.

"Really," Cara said. "You have no fears now. All you will have to do in San Francisco is appear in one of these beautiful gowns, look at the man of your choice through those magnificent, long dark eyelashes of yours, and you will be the toast of the town."

"Would it were so," Catalina said. "All I know is this." She spread her hands to indicate the town and the cantina of the same name. "I wish I had your upbringing."

"Actually it was very dull."

"But you know how to conduct yourself. You know all the little rules."

"Yes, I know which fork to use, but not long ago my ancestors ate their meat with their fingers," Cara said, laughing. "See here, if you're concerned about the teeny little rules of etiquette, that can be quickly corrected."

"I would appreciate your help," Catalina said.

"Catalina!" came a roar from the cantina.

Catalina looked toward Osa's voice. "It is so difficult to talk here."

"We can go to my room at the boardinghouse," Cara said.

Osa was still calling for Catalina when they went out the back door, giggling together at the deception. They spent a lovely midday in Cara's room, and the talk was not all about ladylike behavior but about girl things and men, and Cara began to get the idea. It was the way Catalina's eyes lowered each time she mentioned her brother.

"Why, Catalina," she said, "you're in love with my brother, aren't you?"

"Oh, no."

"Now, now."

"Ah, such a beautiful man."

"Cameron?" Cara asked. "Well, I suppose my proximity to him might make me see him differently."

"Not that there is any possibility—" Catalina said.

"Not? I have seen him look at you."

"It could never be. He is a laird and I . . ." She paused.

"Osa told me only this morning that he can trace his ancestry back to Cortés, himself," Cara said. "I, for one, would be proud to have you as a sister."

Without warning Catalina burst into tears. Cara came to her and held her, whispering nothings until the sudden cascade stopped and Catalina, wet-eyed, looked at her and said, "I will always remember with great joy that which you just said."

"I meant it," Cara said.

"But you do not know. I am not Osa Carranza's daughter." Then it tumbled out, the words sounding so acid that Cara was sure that they must have scalded Catalina's throat, and when she was finished, Cara hugged her and wiped her eyes.

"That does not change my opinion of you a whit," Cara said. "Now, as far as anyone else is concerned, you are Osa's daughter, and you have proud Spanish blood in you."

Cara was thinking. She'd been deeply touched by Catalina's obvious mental agony. The admission that had come from the tortured girl had endeared her to Cara even more.

"This is what we are going to do," she said, making her decision, leaping to her feet. She outlined her plan, and Catalina found it nice to dream, if only for a little while, knowing in her heart that it would come to nothing.

Meanwhile Osa had sent a boy to look for Catalina. When the boy came back and told him that the Widow Brown had reported that Catalina was in the room of the Scottish lady, laughing and talking, Osa nodded. That was good. It was very good for Catalina to be talking and laughing with a real lady. It would help to prepare her for society in San

Francisco. He could, after all, handle the work for that afternoon without her.

The afternoon stretched on. Lucky finished his job, collected his pay, took a quick bath in the inside horse trough, put on clean clothes, and, as the sun was going down, headed toward the cantina, looking forward to his one beer for the day and to a bowl of Osa's chili. Bowen and Cameron, dusty and sweaty from an unsuccessful pursuit of the elusive mountain deer, were seated at a table at the back. The usual crowd was there, meaning most of the Anglo residents and several of the Spanish citizens. Osa was running back and forth from tables to bar, looking a bit harried.

Cara timed the entrance well. She waited until there was a little lull, as it sometimes happens in a saloon or a restaurant, when for some reason everyone stops talking at once.

They came in side by side; one a splendid, dark-haired beauty in a powder-puff-blue evening gown, full, ornate, cut just low enough to be only slightly daring; and a vision in black lace and silk, a white rose in her auburn hair. They paused just inside the door.

"Madre de Dios," Osa croaked as he glanced up, looked away, and jerked his eyes back, as one does at times when the first sight of beauty is too strong for the frail senses and needs a millisecond for adjustment.

Zelma Clemmons smiled with pleasure and then giggled, thinking that every man in the place had suddenly become a flycatcher, all male mouths having dropped open in awe.

Osa, smiling so widely that it showed his gums, a tear of pure joy in his left eye, came running around the counter, bar cloth folded over his left arm, bowed deeply, and said, "Ladies, welcome to my cantina. If you will follow me, please . . ."

Cara nodded imperiously. Catalina had to try hard to stifle a giggle. She matched Cara's ladylike walk, head high, as Osa, the proudest man in New Mexico Territory, led his daughter and her lovely friend to a table, wiped it quickly with the bar cloth, and pulled a chair for Cara first, then for Catalina.

Cameron's mouth was still open. Bowen, feeling not a little pride himself, said, "If I were a surgeon, I could give you a full oral examination."

Cameron's mouth snapped shut. Lucky was still enrapt, his mind doing flip-flops. He'd seen Cara only as the Scottish lady, a beautiful vision that was only passing through to ornament the barrenness for a time. Now, seeing her in the Spanish gown, she seemed so much a part of the surroundings, blending in, his hope soared up like fire, only to smash itself down against the same old arguments having to do with her status and his status, and his income as stable keeper and smithy.

Cameron's reactions were along similiar lines. He had not been able to get Catalina out of his mind. He had told himself time and again that his thoughts of taking her to Scotland with him were foolish, that this girl, so self-possessed and beautiful in the American West, would be nothing more than an odd, out-of-place ornament in the hills of Scotland. Now, seeing her in Cara's dress—for he recognized it—seeing her as she would look seated at his own table, he made a decision. She would be his. That was it. That was final. She would be his not just for a stolen moment on the banks of a river in New Mexico but forever.

Bowen rose, went to the table, bowed to Catalina and Cara. "I thank you both," he said, "for making of this ordinary evening something quite special."

"Thank you," Cara said.

"But these are gowns designed with dancing in mind," Bowen said. He turned and thundered, "Cameron Lockhart, did you not bring the pipes with ye?"

"Does a true Scot ever travel without his pipes?" Cameron asked.

"Then fetch them, and hurry," Bowen shouted, "for I have the music in me, and my toe is already tapping."

Cameron played first, the skirl and thunder of the pipes filling the cantina, causing expressions of surprise on some faces but starting toes to tap. Zelma and Mack leapt up and began to do a respectable reel. Bowen whirled his daughter, then Catalina. Osa, watching his beautiful daughter, overflowed a glass of beer and did not even curse at the waste. Then it was Bowen with the pipes, and he was a master, causing the aged cedar rafters to ring with the gaiety of a Highland fling, nodding with interest as Cameron approached Catalina and began to teach her the steps.

Cara went to Lucky's table, took his hand, and said gaily, "Only I am without a partner." Lucky shambled to his feet and stumbled a bit, but it wasn't long before he felt as if his feet had sprouted wings, and he made up for his lack of skill and grace with an enthusiasm that left Cara breathless.

It was, all in all, a grand evening during which Bowen got happily drunk and played the pipes until he was red in the face, and then, sadly, it was over and Catalina was in her own bed and Cara in hers, both a bit let down. Catalina, who had allowed herself to dream, was the most pained by the silence after the gala evening, and she cried herself to sleep, only to dream that Cameron was calling to her. She stirred, heard her name being whispered through the barred, open window, held the sheets to her throat, and sat up to see Cameron's form outlined against a starry sky.

"I must speak with you," Cameron whispered. "It won't wait. Can you come out?"

She thought about it. She could possibly sneak out without waking Osa, since he had joined in the celebration and was probably sleeping quite soundly. Still, it was a risk.

"Wait for me by the stream," she whispered back.

She dressed quickly, leaving off the petticoats, and tiptoed, shoes in hand, into the cantina and outside by the front door. Cameron was standing by the stream, and when she approached, he ran to meet her and took her two hands in his.

"I will not keep you out long in the night air," he said, "so I will come to the point quickly. I will not leave here without you. You are going back to Scotland with me, as my wife."

Catalina's heart leapt with joy, and then the acid sadness came quickly as he bent to kiss her. She took that one kiss, took it to have and to hold and to treasure, and then she pushed him away.

"You will not say no," he ordered.

"Not I," she whispered.

"Good."

"You will say no, Cameron, and I will understand."

"Don't be enigmatic," he said, bending to kiss her again.

She told him then. It didn't come tumbling out as it had with Cara, but it came, and with each revelation she felt Cameron's hands stiffen, and then he dropped her hands and stood as if stricken.

"So you see, I release you from your proposal," she said finally.

It was a heavy blow. "Well," he said. Then, "Well, perhaps—"

"You do not have to say anything," she said, turning to run back to the cantina. Cameron stood beside the stream for a long, long time before making his way to the boardinghouse and to bed. It was, after all, too much. He was a man of responsible holdings, and he lived among people whom he liked and respected, a moral, hard-nosed people who would not understand one of their peers marrying the daughter of a Mexican whore.

Cara had no nighttime callers. She slept well and was at table when Cameron came down for breakfast, looking as if he hadn't slept at all.

"Have you ever seen anything more lovely than Catalina was last night?" Cara asked brightly after exchanging morning greetings.

"I'm going to speak to Smith today," Cameron said. "If he is not ready to take the coach into Socorro within a day or two, we will rent horses and ride down."

"Isn't this rather sudden?" she asked, wondering what in the world had happened to make Cameron so morose and testy.

"At least I will ride down," he said. "If you still insist on resisting good sense and the best advice given to you by me, your legal guardian, then stay. Perhaps Osa can find a place for you at the cantina where you can dress up like a Mexican prostitute and dazzle cowboys and sheepherders."

Cara resisted the temptation to flare back at him. Something had happened to him. He was not hitting out at her so much as at something—perhaps even himself.

"Cameron, would you like to tell me what's bothering you?" she asked, placing her hand over his.

He jerked his hand away, but his voice was softer. "It's time for us to go home, sister. There is nothing here for us."

She nodded rather sadly, but he missed that aspect of it, so lost was he in his own misery. True, she was thinking, there seemed to be nothing there for either of them. Her own father didn't want her to stay. And the most intriguing man she'd ever met could hardly bring himself to say a civil word to her.

"All right, Cameron," she said. "I will begin my packing straight away."

When Bowen came straggling down, looking a bit red-eyed, it was Cameron who made the announcement.

"Ah, but I'll be sorry to see you go," Bowen said.

Then ask me to stay, Cara was thinking.

"Do you need any help in preparing?" Bowen asked.

"No thank you," Cara said.

"I'll ride down the mountain with ye, of course," Bowen said.

"Kind of you," Cameron said.

"And before you go," Bowen said, "we must have the grandest gathering of all to bid ye farewell." He turned to Cara. "It would pleasure me, Daughter, to see you dressed once more in that gown of Catalina's."

"I think not," Cara said coldly.

"Oh? Well, then," Bowen said. "But ye will, both of you, allow me to stage a send-off party for ye?"

"If you must," Cameron said.

"Such enthusiasm," Bowen said, but he ate quickly and went to talk with Osa about making some special preparations, maybe a venison stew instead of chili, and then made the rounds of the town, inviting all and sundry to join them.

Cameron found Lucky sitting on the rail fence of the stable corral, looking a bit glum. Yes, Lucky agreed, it was time for another run to Socorro. Tomorrow would do just fine.

"Too bad you can't stay longer," Lucky said, thinking of how Cara's eyes had sparkled when they were dancing. And, he thought, too bad he wasn't something more than a failed sheepherder. His luck was holding, all right. Not even the sight of the coach could cheer him. Something would probably happen to it, too, and if it didn't, what the hell did it mean? He could run the coach up and down the hill until he wore the iron off the rims and he wouldn't be any richer, wouldn't be any closer to being the kind of man who could speak out to a woman like Cara Lockhart.

Chapter Thirteen

All day long the nameless, smiling, buxom woman who manned Osa's kitchen was busy, and it seemed to her that every time she turned around there was someone else underfoot. The word of Bowen's farewell party had, it seemed, spread, almost magically, to those occasional visitors to Dos Caballos who roamed the hills in the company of sheep and cows and burros. Luke Malloy came in early, contributing a lamb and insisting to the kitchen matron that he was, without doubt, the West's finest cooker of leg of lamb Mexicana, meaning that he used much pepper.

Heck Logan contributed a piece of veal and borrowed ingredients from the kitchen to baste and flavor it, drafting several urchins of the town to turn the spit in the backyard behind the cantina. A steady stream of cakes and pies—and this was perhaps the best indication that Dos Caballos had taken the two young Lockharts to its heart, the use of precious sugar and dried apples and flour—poured into the cantina.

Several of the men began the party early, and this didn't displease Osa. He was kept busy during the late afternoon and early evening pouring and serving, and the cash box took on a healthy weight. He assumed that Catalina was busy with her own preparations. After having seen his daughter dressed up and acting like a proper lady, he was willing to do the work himself and look forward to the reward of seeing her again as she'd looked on the previous night. He didn't bother her at all. If he had gone to Catalina's room, he would have been a puzzled man, to see her lying limply on her stomach across her bed, her face blank, her eyes devoid of their usual sparkle.

Lucky went down to the cantina just after dark. The place was more crowded than he'd ever seen it. It took a while just to make the rounds of the room and shake hands and say, "Been a while. How's things over, or up, or down, at such-and-such." He was pleased that there seemed to be a lot of interest in the coach ride down to Socorro and had to turn down several who had decided, perhaps in the spirit of the evening, that it might be fun to go along on the trip the next day. The coach was full already, and he didn't want to put passengers on top because of the mountain roads and the fact that he had to use one team of horses all the way and didn't want to overload them.

The Lockhart family arrived as a group, Cara in blue, more beautiful, Lucky thought, than he'd ever seen her. Cameron wore a somewhat somber tweed outfit, but Bowen was splendiferous in his Black Watch tartan. He didn't bristle when he was greeted with whistles and cheers. He was carrying the pipes, and even as Cameron and Cara made their way to the table reserved for them, he first downed a healthy shot of whiskey and then began to pipe a quiet and plaintive melody, or, at least, as quiet and plaintive a melody as can be played on the bagpipes.

Cameron, quite subdued, looked around, nodded, and smiled as people spoke. He did not see Catalina.

Cara said, "Looking for someone?" She smiled archly, unaware of Cameron's chaotic thoughts.

Osa had given strict orders that not one bite of food was to be served before eight o'clock. He wanted to give this, the largest crowd he'd ever had in the cantina, time to soak up some happiness in the form of his stock-in-trade before they dulled their thirst with food.

Luke Malloy was trying to do a Highland fling and succeeded only in looking like a demented dervish. Two ranchers of Scottish blood were singing along with Bowen's playing, their voices not all bad. Cara was wondering why Catalina hadn't joined the party. She excused herself and made her way to Catalina's room. Catalina was dressed in white, and Cara smiled when she saw her, for the pure white was quite complimentary to the girl. It took a bit of coaxing to get Catalina out of her room, and she came only when Cara said, "Whatever is wrong with you? Everyone in this part of New Mexico Territory is waiting to see how beautiful you are. Your father can't keep his eyes off the doorway, waiting for you to appear."

Catalina kept her eyes down as Cara led her to the table, then looked up once, to see Cameron looking at her with an unreadable expression. She felt a stab of pain. For a moment she mourned what, in a fairy-tale world, might have been, and then her natural vibrancy, her youth, her pride—even if, had she been asked by someone who *knew,* she would have said that she had no more pride—came to her aid and she blazed a smile at Bowen, turned her head to examine the room, and became Catalina, flirting and speaking to all the men who, at one time or another, were customers of the cantina.

Bowen was standing at the inside end of the bar, the point most distant from the door. Lucky was near him but not too near, since the volume of sound issuing from the pipes was quite something up close. It was nearing eight o'clock. Zelma went back to the kitchen, taking a couple of Dos Caballos matrons with her to help serve the food. The cantina was filled with music and talk and laughter. No one noticed that the two guests of honor, Cameron and Cara, were not joining in the gaiety.

It was the sound of Bowen's bagpipes that drew Craw Maddock toward the cantina. He'd decided to take a look at Dos Caballos, tired of being alone in the mountains, and once he'd ridden into town, he heard this ungodly noise and had to see who was making it. He sat his horse outside the cantina, noting from the horses tied to the hitch rail that there were a lot of people inside, and tried to figure it out. He knew that it wasn't a good idea for him to go inside, lest he be recognized. It wouldn't do, with what he had planned, for a lot of people to know that he'd been seen in Dos Caballos. But his curiosity got the better of him. He walked onto the board porch and peered in through a window. The place was crowded. He could not see Bowen from that angle, but he heard what he figured must be some kind of music and saw people dancing. He also saw, seated at a table, the redhead that had interested him in Socorro, the fancy woman from the Old Country, and he licked his lips and started thinking thoughts.

* * *

Chunk Wilson had started thinking thoughts two days previously. His thoughts about Maddock were not kind. His thoughts about Lucky Smith and the Socorro stage were sanguine. He had, he decided, waited long enough. Since everything else regarding his plans to build a stage-line empire was at a standstill, there was one positive thing he could do, and that was to make it clear to one and all, forever, that Chunk Wilson was not going to stand idly by and let some sheepherder go into competition with him on his own front doorstep. He called together four of his best men, men who would ask no questions and would follow orders, men who were more than handy with guns. By riding hard, he was camped five miles outside Dos Caballos on the night of the farewell party. He had seen the road down the hill, and he thought that any man who wanted to drive a stage on that route with any sort of regularity was crazy, but that was beside the point. The point was that the Dos Caballos stage had made its last run. He'd send a man into town in the morning to try to get an idea when Smith was going to take the coach down the hill again.

Maddock had been in the mountains too long. The scent of Osa's home brew, wafting through the window, was too much for him. He pulled his hat low and adjusted his .44 on his hip and pushed open the doors. He was not noticed. The party was really going now, with half a dozen men clomping and stomping in the middle of the floor to the damnedest sound Maddock had ever heard. He made his way to the near end of the bar and, when Osa came, smiling, ordered beer. He gulped half of the beer quickly and turned, leaning back on the bar to watch the woman in blue at the table at the back of the room. She was smiling and talking to a Mex girl, who wasn't bad herself. When the beer was gone, Maddock croaked, "Whiskey, bring the bottle." Osa grinned. Now that was the kind of drinking man he liked, even if he was a stranger who'd never been in the cantina before.

Zelma came out of the kitchen carrying a huge platter holding a steaming leg of lamb. "All right, everybody," she said, and her voice was enough to quiet both Bowen and the talking and laughing, "what we're gonna do is set up everything on the bar, and you-all jest he'p yourselves."

Lucky's mouth began to water as the food poured from the kitchen. The aroma of Heck Logan's spit-cooked veal was the finest scent he'd ever smelled, except, maybe, for the perfume Cara Lockhart wore. He hitched up his pants and reached for a plate. He looked down the bar, planning his attack, and looked straight into the eyes of a man whose identity, for a moment, escaped him. Then it came to him. He felt a little tingle of alarm, because the last time he'd seen that man he'd been invited to get into a gunfight, and then he'd been pounded upon rather severely.

Maddock held Lucky's eyes for a few moments and then looked away. Lucky checked around. Dos Caballos was not a gun-toting town. A couple of the ranchers or cowhands had come wearing irons, but their pistols and belts were hanging up behind the bar, shed for comfort and ease of dancing. Maddock, however, had his .44 hanging on his hip, low and dangerous. Lucky shrugged mentally. The man would be a fool to start something with around twenty men in the cantina.

Maddock probably wouldn't have started anything. He was reckless but not really a fool. It was just that he'd been making up for lost time, hitting hard a bottle of Osa's watered whiskey, and he'd never seen a Scot in kilts before. From his position at the bar he'd been blocked from Bowen, and it was not until people began to mill around and prepare to attack the generous spread of food that he saw the Scot. He blinked, whiskey glass halfway to his mouth, finished the motion, took whiskey into his mouth, and then blew it out in an explosion of uncontrollable laughter.

He couldn't stop it. He dropped the glass. It didn't break but rolled a little. He bent, roaring. He slapped his thigh. He looked at the Scot, eyes streaming with laughter-induced tears.

"Woo-ha," Luke Malloy yelped, beginning to roll up his sleeves, anticipating the fun. He knew from experience what Bowen Lockhart's reaction was going to be.

"Bowen . . . now, Bowen," Lucky said, taking Bowen's arm.

Bowen cast one look at the table where Cameron and Cara sat, as if wondering whether the activity he had in mind was proper in front of his daughter.

If Maddock had shut up, the moment might have passed. But he couldn't. He pointed a finger. It shook with his laughter.

"Bowen, dadgum it, not before we *eat*," Lucky yelped as Bowen jerked away from his hand on Bowen's arm.

"Whose side you gonna be on?" Luke asked the man next to him. "We cain't all gang up on one stranger. That ain't even enough for ole Bowen."

"Bowen." Lucky moaned as Bowen stalked toward the laughing Maddock.

Maddock didn't recognize the man who had coldcocked him in Socorro until Bowen was halfway down the bar. His laughter died in his throat. He looked around nervously. He was a stranger in a strange land, outnumbered about twenty to one, not counting women. His reaction came from sudden fright, a quick change from one emotion to another, from Osa's watered whiskey, and from his frustration at having wasted days and nights camping alone in the mountains. His .44 appeared in his hand.

Cara screamed, "Father!"

Bowen didn't pause. There was a happy grin on his face. He couldn't think of anyone he'd rather have laugh at the tartan of the Black Watch than the man who'd manhandled his daughter. This was, he was thinking, going to be rather enjoyable.

The explosion of Maddock's Colt rattled glasses on the shelves, filled the cantina. There was the sudden odor of burned powder. There was a momentary silence as Bowen, jerked halfway around by the impact of a heavy .44-caliber slug, crashed against the bar and then began to slide to the floor.

Lucky leaned forward, but his feet seemed to be frozen. The transition from party time to violence had been too much. Only Cara reacted instantly, leaping from her chair to fly, skirts swirling, toward the falling Bowen.

Craw Maddock knew that he was in big trouble. He moved the muzzle of his Colt back and forth, just waiting for someone to try to jump him. He saw the movement of blue, Cara, and then she was only a couple of feet from him, running toward the man in the funny skirt who was now slumped on the floor.

Maddock didn't have time to reason it all out. His action was instinctive. If he'd had time, he would have rationalized that since he was in trouble already, he might as well take full advantage of it. He was, and had always been, an opportunist. And opportunity was moving past him, a blur of blue, as he reached out his arm and caught Cara by the hair and jerked her to him. Cara let out of yelp of pain and tried to turn, fingers clawed to reach for his eyes, and he clipped her lightly on the temple with the barrel of his gun, laying it on longways so as not to kill her or cut her. She wobbled a little and he was holding her to his chest, his Colt out.

"Don't nobody move," he said, backing toward the door. By now he'd had time to figure out that he might as well be hunted for getting something he wanted, as well as for gunning down the dude in the skirt. He was licking his lips in anticipation. In the face of his gun there was no movement in the room as he backed out the door and then shot once, aiming high through the door so that the slug thudded into one of the old, darkened cedar beams.

He threw Cara into the saddle. She was half limp, dazed, so that he had to hold her there as he swung up behind the saddle and got the horse in motion. He had himself a good feel of soft breast even while he was on the main street of Dos Caballos, and then he was headed south, making pretty good time, for he had a stout horse who was not heavily burdened by Cara's additional weight. For a moment, he wondered, what the hell had happened. There was gold at stake. He'd killed the man with the gold, and now he might never find it. Then he brightened. Surely the dude would have told his own kids about it. He might be able to get the secret of Lockhart's gold from this girl, who was beginning to protest.

"Shut up," he hissed into her ear. "Don't make me pistol-whip you again, 'cause I might not be able to keep from hurting you, seeing as we're moving along right smart."

"Get your filthy hand off me," Cara said as Maddock got another feel of breast.

"All right, take it easy," he said. "You ain't gonna get hurt. I jest needed a ticket out of that place, that's all." Lying didn't bother him a bit.

Lucky was the first one out. He grabbed a horse—he thought it might be Heck's—and was heading south when he realized he didn't have a gun. It took five minutes to ride to the stable and get his old Navy Colt and strap it on, and then he was headed south again. Fortunately there was a good moon, and there in the highlands it made things so bright that he could spot where a horse carrying a double load had taken the road leading down the hill. He knew that he had the advantage of a horse that could travel faster, and that he knew the country. He'd just have to be sure that he spotted it when Maddock left the trail—if he did, and he probably would.

Lucky wasn't a praying man. He'd prayed a lot when his wife was alive, mostly because she liked it, but what had it gotten him? But for some reason he found himself reciting the Lord's Prayer as he rode, eyes on the trail, spotting the heavy indentation of Maddock's horse now and then. He was reciting the Lord's Prayer because he couldn't put his feelings into words, was not willing to face the fear that Maddock would simply kill Cara and dump her now that she'd served the purpose of helping him get out of the cantina. Nor would he allow himself to think of other things that could happen. He just wouldn't give Maddock time to find a spot where he could have his way with Cara.

The moon got higher. Maddock was sticking to the road and had wound up and around two ridges to a point about five miles south of Dos Caballos. Soon the road would turn southwest and climb out of the canyon. Lucky was riding hard, so that he missed the point where Maddock had left the trail and was fifteen minutes up the road before he turned around and began to backtrack. By the time he had located the point where Maddock's tracks led down toward the creek, he figured he'd wasted at least half an hour.

Long enough to give Maddock time to prepare. He was looking forward to it, but he wanted to be able to see what he was doing. He had made his way through a brushy canyon into a small, secluded glen beside the stream, so that he would be able to wash up afterward—a man had to think of things like that, after all. He knew that there'd be people chasing him, but he didn't figure those sheepherders from Dos Caballos would be able to track at night. He didn't need much time, just enough to build a little fire within a circle of big boulders—that would make it hard to spot—and put his blanket on the ground. He had the girl's hands and legs tied.

Cara's head ached. She wasn't even free to rub the spot where a knot had formed on her temple. She was sprawled on the blanket and she watched with growing fear as Maddock built his fire and then walked toward her.

"Now, I'd advise you," he said, "to make it easy on yourself. You fight and I fight, but there ain't no need for that." He reached down, seized her bodice, and ripped downward. "Damn," he said, finding that cloth doesn't rip all that easy. He pulled his knife and began to operate on dress and undergarments. Cara yelped and he slapped her, just a little bit.

Lucky saw the glow of the fire. He couldn't believe that the man would have the arrogance to build a fire, not with people chasing him. He dismounted and snubbed the reins to a bush and looked around. The moon sailed serenely overhead. There was a hint of a night breeze. A pack of coyotes were enjoying the moon from a far ridge. Up ahead he heard a horse blow through his lips, and he began to creep forward. He knew the area. Up ahead there was a little clearing surrounded by boulders, and the last time he'd hunted through there, there'd been a bit of grass growing. It was a pretty good place.

Lucky approached the fire from the high side, away from the creek. He had to make his way through dense, thorny brush and he didn't accomplish that without some small letting of blood, but he kept quiet and moved slowly. He respected Maddock's gun. Dead, he wouldn't be of any use to Cara. He climbed a rocky slope and peered over a boulder and flushed, even as he whispered, "Dadgum," under his breath.

Maddock had bared Cara to the waist. He had her staked out with her arms and legs spread, like, some told, Indians did to their victims, usually on an anthill or in the full glare of the desert sun. She was bucking and struggling, sounds that were a mixture of outrage, anger, and fear coming from her mouth. Her dress was a wreck and was becoming even more so as Maddock, mouth open, tongue in one corner, began to work on the lower section of her voluminous garments, ripping away sections of petticoat with the aid of the knife, revealing her lower limbs encased in stockings.

Lucky's hesitation came from two sources. First, he was shocked to the core of his being that a man could be so low as to do such a thing to a helpless, struggling woman and not be an Indian; secondly, because he was discovering as he leveled his old Navy Colt at Maddock, that he was not the kind of man to shoot another from ambush, even under dire provocation. He thought it out and Maddock was becoming impatient now, rending away all but a pair of fluffy white bloomers. The only thing to do, Lucky felt, was go down and confront this animal as if he were a man.

His luck held. He was easing his way down over a big boulder, about ten feet above the ground level of the little glen, when he slipped and with a great sound of sliding rock went pounding down, bouncing, to land on his back in the sparse grass. He felt his lungs spasm, pumping for air, and it took him a while to catch his breath, which came out in great, noisy gasps.

Maddock leapt to his feet, pistol in hand. He looked around to see if there was anyone else, and all was silent, save for Lucky's gasping.

"Well, what have we here?" Maddock asked.

"Maddock," Lucky gasped, "you give that lady her clothes this minute."

Maddock laughed. He lifted his pistol as Lucky struggled to his knees, feeling around in the grass for his own weapon, which, his luck holding, he had dropped. In the firelight, Cara could see Maddock's face, and she could see his trigger finger tightening.

"That's lovely," she said. "Just lovely. What a brave man you are. You were about to show me that you are a man, and now you're going to shoot an unarmed man who is hurt."

Maddock let his finger relax. "Shut up," he said, but he was looking at her. Her bare breasts were so white. He licked his lips.

Cara was desperate. For the moment she wasn't concerned about what had been and what was going to happen to her. She was thinking only of Lucky. She felt like weeping in frustration, but not because he was clumsy. That didn't matter. She felt that he had to care for her; otherwise, he wouldn't be out here all alone facing the gun of a murderer. "I might even have enjoyed it," she said, "but how can anyone enjoy it when the man is a coward who shoots unarmed men?"

She was praying, "Do something, Lucky, for God's sake, do something."

Lucky couldn't find his gun.

"Well," Craw said, "it don't matter much, anyhow, but if you want to see me take this sheepherder, we'll give you a little show. Stand up, sheepherder."

"I can't find my gun," Lucky said.

Maddock said a few choice words, bent, picked up a blazing branch, and walked toward Lucky.

"Here it is," Lucky said.

"Right," Maddock said. "Now come over here where the little lady will have a good view."

Lucky walked, putting his Colt back in his holster, since Maddock's .44 was aimed at his belly. Maddock went to one side of the fire, Lucky to the other, standing about twenty feet apart.

Lucky sneaked a look at Cara. The firelight played over her creamy white torso, over the flattened mounds of her breasts. He had difficulty breathing. He looked back at Maddock and felt something—hate, maybe—something that began to straighten him, to fill him. He felt something like a growl form in his throat.

"I'm gonna give you a fair draw, sheepherder," Maddock said, supremely confident, knowing that he had the fastest draw he'd ever seen, a draw that had been the last sight on earth for over a dozen men. He put the .44 back in the holster, shrugged to loosen his muscles, posing for Cara. If she wanted to see a man in action, he'd show her this first, and then a couple of other things.

"Anytime you're ready, go for it," Maddock said, grinning to show his teeth.

Lucky felt something shoot stingingly into his stomach, felt it spread until his body glowed. His eyes narrowed. He was breathing shallowly but evenly.

Cara was holding her breath, her eyes darting back and forth from one shadowy, firelit figure to the other, praying, "Please, please, please."

She gasped then as Lucky's Navy Colt seemed to suddenly materialize in his hand with a quick movement.

For the rest of his life he would never know how he did it. He had, like most Westerners, practiced a little, but a sheepherder and a blacksmith doesn't spend too much time practicing the fast draw. He'd killed his share of rattlesnakes, and sometimes he'd had to be pretty quick to get the snake before it got him, but he'd never faced a man with his life, depending on the quickness of his draw and the accuracy of his first shot.

It was accuracy that did it. Two guns boomed as one. Then silence. Both shadowy, firelit figures stood, but Maddock's neck was wrong. His head was tilted far back. Lucky stood, Colt extended, and watched as Maddock, like a tall tree, leaned backward and fell.

Cara caught a look at Maddock's face. Where his nose had been there was a gaping cavity that first filled with blood and then flowed. His legs began to move, his heels beating a dull tattoo on the earth. Lucky still stood, not really believing that he was alive. Cara screamed and turned her head. The sound brought Lucky out of it. He holstered his Colt and walked around the fire to gaze down at the dead man's noseless, bloody face. He'd been aiming for the forehead.

Cara's voice was soft, tired-sounding. "Lucky? Lucky?"

He turned, walked to stand at her feet, and was filled with a sense of sheer beauty, with no carnal thoughts, just an appreciation of beauty. He'd seen only one woman naked in his life, his Maddy, and she'd been beautiful, in a stringy, skinny sort of way, but this was sheer loveliness.

"Please release me, Lucky," Cara said.

"Yeah, sure," Lucky said, unable to take his eyes off her beauty.

"Lucky!"

He knelt, reaching for his knife. He was a little ashamed of himself, tried to pull the blanket up to hide her nakedness while he cut the ropes.

"Never mind," she said, "just cut me loose."

He first cut the ropes that held her feet, removed them from her ankles, feeling the shape of her leg, her foot. Then he cut the ropes that held her hands, and she sat up, not trying to grab for cover, and her breasts formed their standing shape, firm and pointed, and he gulped and tried to turn his head but couldn't.

Cara said, "Is there something I could wear?"

"The blanket," Lucky said. Then, "Wait, let me have a look." He found Maddock's slicker and she stood, and he held it as she slipped her arms into it.

"Thank you, Lucky," she said, turning to face him. "Thank you for coming after me."

"Oh, there'd have been others," he said, not knowing what to say.

"But not before it was too late," she said. "You came. You got here in time."

"Yeah, well," Lucky said. "Maybe we better go back now."

Suddenly Cara remembered. "My father!" she gasped.

"I don't know," Lucky said. "I ran out right after Maddock pulled you out the door."

Chapter Fourteen

Chunk Wilson didn't actually hear the two shots that came almost as one, but the sound awoke him so that he lay there for a minute, trying to figure out what he'd heard.

"Shots, Mr. Wilson," one of his men said. "Came from up the creek a ways."

"Someone scaring off coyotes," another man said.

It was getting on toward dawn, so Wilson didn't try to go back to sleep. He had a man make some coffee and was on the road as first light came.

"What are you going to do with him?" Cara asked. She was bundled into the stiff, hot slicker with only her bloomers under it. Lucky was ready to give her a hand to get on Maddock's horse.

"We'll send someone down to bury him," Lucky said. "I guess we'd best go see about Bowen."

His luck held. He gained the road, leading the way at first light, just in time to run head-on into Chunk Wilson and four men with guns. Wilson recognized Lucky immediately.

"You fire some shots a while back?" Wilson asked.

"Not me," Lucky said. He knew that Maddock worked for Wilson, and he didn't want to have trouble with Wilson and four men, not with Cara along.

Wilson looked at the horse Cara was riding. "Looks like Craw Maddock's horse," he said.

Lucky swallowed. It was Cara, sensing Lucky's concern, who said, "Lots of horses look alike."

"And lots of saddles have C. M, for Craw Maddock, burned into the skirt," Wilson said.

The conversation was taking place with Cara and Lucky sitting their horses facing north. Wilson's horse was out in front of those of his four men. They had just passed the point where Craw Maddock had left the road when they had heard the sound of Lucky and Cara coming toward the trail and had turned. Heck Logan's horse was not old and placid like Lucky's own Jughead. He was ready for action, especially action that would take him back toward town, where there would be oats and water at the stable corral. He was fidgeting and moving forward a few inches at a time, closing the space between Lucky and Wilson.

"I think maybe I did hear gunshots," Wilson said. "I think maybe this woman is riding Maddock's horse because Craw isn't in any condition to ride it. And I think the only way a sheepherder like you could put Craw out of action would be to shoot him from behind."

"Lucky wouldn't do a thing like that," Cara said.

"Cara, hush," Lucky said. he grinned at Wilson. "Now, Mr. Wilson, I'll admit some questions need answering, but this lady has had a pretty bad experience, and I'm sure you'll agree with me that we need to get her back to town where she can get some clothes and have a doctor look at her." That there was no doctor in Dos Caballos didn't matter. Lucky was grasping at straws.

"Let's just ride back down toward the creek the way you came and see if we don't find something interesting," Wilson said. He had the owner and operator of the Dos Caballos Stage Company before him, and he wasn't going to let him get away. On the other hand, he didn't want to simply kill Smith with the girl as a witness. He edged his horse off to one side a little as Lucky's mount jerked, and took three quick steps forward before Lucky reined him in.

"Or, Smith," Wilson said, "there's another way. You can admit you back-shot Maddock and stole his horse, and then we'll see how you do face-to-face with a man.''

Lucky could feel death in the air. He had faced one gunman and, calling up reserves from inside, talents he didn't even know he had, he'd survived. However, he had no illusions about his skill with a gun, at least not to the point of thinking that he could survive an encounter with five men. He was quite near Wilson now, and he knew that his time was running out. He kicked the horse and shouted at the same time. As the horse leapt forward he threw himself off and onto Wilson's horse behind the saddle, accomplishing the move, to his surprise, without disaster, and he had his Colt pressed hard into Wilson's neck.

"Now, Mr. Wilson, we don't want trouble. We just want to get on back to town and see about this lady's father, who was shot down without a weapon in his hands by your friend, Maddock.''

"Easy," Wilson said, both to Lucky and to the men who faced him, as Lucky reached down with one hand and pulled Wilson's horse around.

"Lucky, look out," Cara cried as one of the men threw the only thing he had to throw, his pistol. The gun took Lucky on the side of the head and he felt the world explode, felt himself falling, landing with a thud that partially cleared his head. Amazingly he'd hung on to his gun. He came to one knee and looked up into the muzzle of Wilson's pistol.

"Good-bye, Mr. Smith," Wilson said, his finger tightening on the trigger. Lucky began to bring his gun up, and it was as if he were moving in slow motion and the Colt weighed a ton. He heard a shot and wondered why he didn't feel dead. He was looking into Wilson's face, and he saw a dark spot appear suddenly on Wilson's forehead.

The shot had come from one of Bowen's dueling pistols. It was in the hand of Cameron, who, seeing Wilson's unmistakable intent to kill Lucky, had stepped quickly from the brush. Beside him, Cara saw a man, naked to the waist save for a bulky bandage, and her heart leapt when she recognized the fighting grin of her father.

A gun spat and the bullet clipped brush near Bowen's head. Lucky was on his feet, and two men faced him, guns leveled. He triggered off two quick shots and felt something whistle a song of near death past his ear, and then he was turning to see Bowen leveling his old Sharps and to hear the resounding bang of the weapon. A man was knocked all the way out of his saddle by the slug that could stop a running buffalo bull and then, in a carol of shots, the fourth man went down from the remaining charged dueling pistol in Cameron's hands.

Then there was silence. A horse blew softly through its lips. Five men were dead, two from Lucky's gun. Cara was pressing her lips together so hard, they were hurting. She looked at Cameron, whose face was white but grim; looked at her father, who grinned at her; looked at Lucky, who blushed.

"There's another one down by the creek," Cara said.

"Maddock?" Bowen asked.

Lucky nodded. He was still a little numb and his head hurt. He lifted a hand and it came away bloody. Cara, seeing it, came off her horse, exposing white bloomers as the slicker parted. She ran to Lucky. "You're hurt."

"Not much," he said.

"I wanted Maddock myself," Bowen grumbled.

Cara stood on tiptoe, looking at the small cut on the side of Lucky's head. "When we get back to town, I'll clean it and treat it," she said.

"Ah, it's not bad," Lucky said.

"Cara," Cameron asked, "are you all right?"

"I'm fine," she said, still fussing over Lucky.

"That outlaw didn't harm you?" Cameron asked.

Lucky was not looking at her. He was staring up at the sky, watching the flight of a couple of buzzards who had probably seen Maddock's body down by the creek and were checking it out. Cara, who had been through a lot, after all, lost her temper. She didn't scream or blush red; the change was inside. How dense, she thought, can a man be? What does a girl have to do to get one of these big, silent types of the American West to speak up?

"The outlaw did not harm me," she said, turning to face Cameron and Bowen, "but Mr. Smith has seen me almost nude, and I call on you, my father and my brother, to see that Mr. Smith does the right thing by me."

"What on earth are ye talking about?" Cameron asked.

Bowen grinned.

"I am speaking of the code of the Scottish highlands," Cara said. "This man has seen my intimate parts." She looked at Bowen, who winked at her. *Ah,* he was thinking, *so the lass has fallen for Lucky, as I suspected.* "Father, you, at least, must know what has to happen now."

"There are two choices, Lucky," Bowen said.

"Now wait a minute," Cameron said. "How did you, ah, lose your clothing, Cara? Did Lucky remove it?"

"No," Lucky said, shocked at the idea. He appealed to Cara with a look.

"No, it was not Mr. Smith who removed them, and to his credit he killed the man who did," Cara said, "Nevertheless, he did see me naked from the waist up." She knew from her father's smile that Bowen understood.

"Well, if he didn't take your clothing—" Cameron said.

"Cameron, where is your sense of Scottish honor?" Bowen asked. "Lucky, as I said, there are two choices." He raised the old Sharps. Lucky wasn't cool enough, was confused enough not to realize that the gun had not been reloaded. "I can shoot you," Bowen said.

"What's the other choice?" Lucky asked, trying to make some sense of this.

"You make an honest woman of my daughter," Bowen said.

"Do what?" Cameron yelled.

"Huh?" Lucky asked.

"Marry the lass," Bowen said.

"Well . . ." Lucky said.

"You absolute lunk," Cara yelled after a strained silence. "Am I so horrible that you'd rather be shot than marry me?"

"Well, I'll be damned," Lucky said, using his allowance of profanity for the year, "if I'd know that that was all it took, I'd have ripped your clothes off weeks ago."

"Lucky?" she asked, taking a step toward him.

"Cara? Dadgum it, I didn't know, didn't dare think—didn't have any hope—"

"Hush," she said, standing on tiptoe to reach his lips.

The Dos Caballos cemetery was across the creek, tucked under a hill. Some of the gravestones were quite old, with Spanish inscriptions carved into the native rock. No one was in the mood to do much work for the five new graves there, so wooden markers had had to do.

Zelma held a Bible and read a couple of verses. Then she said, "We don't even know the names of some of these cusses, Lord, but they's in your hands now, or in the hands of the devil, whatever. We done our duty to human flesh, and now it's up to you."

Cara and Lucky were in Bowen's room at the boardinghouse. Lucky was sporting a new, clean, huge bandage that almost covered his head, and he didn't dare remove it, although his wound was only a scratch on top of a growing bump on the side of his head. Bowen was making faces and groaning a bit as Cara changed the bandage that was tied across his chest.

"Aye, that's a proper lass," Bowen said. "In the old days, Scottish women knew their business when it came to treating war wounds."

"This one doesn't look serious," Cara said.

"Serious? It's damned painful."

"But I don't think it touched bone. Clean in and clean out."

"I'll have a devil of a time regaining strength in this left arm," Bowen said. "It might be that I'll have to move in with my daughter and her new husband so that she can care for me."

"In the room at the top of the stable?" Lucky asked. The euphoria of knowing that Cara loved him was being diluted by reality. Where would he house a wife, a wife like Cara?

"That would not be cozy," Bowen said. "It has occurred to me, my future son-in-law, that you need to improve your prospects somewhat." He waited until Cara had tied the bandage and then sat up with a grunt or two. "Speaking of which, it would seem, with the untimely death of Mr. Wilson, that there might be a stagecoach line for sale. Considering that you have some experience, and that Socorro, or perhaps even Santa Fe, might offer more comfortable accommodations to my daughter than a room over a stable, I think we will consider making an offer for the late Mr. Wilson's holdings."

"With what?" Lucky asked, spreading his hands.

"There's that matter, too," Bowen said. "No daughter of mine would ever go to the marriage bed without a proper dowry."

Lucky was silent, wondering where a desert rat like Bowen planned to get enough money not only to buy a stage line but to buy a proper house for his daughter.

"Cara, would you please call Cameron?" Bowen asked.

When Cameron was in the room, looking a bit pale, a bit forlorn, Bowen said, "My boy, you know where I store a few items of some value up at my claim, do you not?"

"I do," Cameron said.

"I would like you to take Mr. Smith and bring those items here, to Dos Caballos, from which point we will load them onto your future brother's coach and take them down to civilization and put them to work."

"I'll be riding that coach, Father," Cameron said, "when it leaves Dos Caballos."

"To my sadness," Bowen said, "but ye're a man grown, and you must do what you must do."

Cara followed Cameron from the room, catching him by the arm and pulling him to a halt, then guiding him into her own room. "What's wrong with you?" she asked.

"Is there something wrong with me?"

"There is. Is it that you had to kill two men?"

He looked away. "I will admit that in the heat of the moment it seemed to be the only way, but since then I have realized that it was definitely the only way to save Lucky's life, and perhaps yours. No, I do not lie awake nights regretting having killed two blackguards."

"What is it, then?" she asked. "Is it that you are undecided about going home?"

"Not in the least," he said. "My place is in Scotland. I have, after all, duties and responsibilities there."

"You're so quiet and pale."

"It's the climate, I suppose."

She took a deep breath. "Could it be Catalina?"

His face darkened and he glared at her. "I will hear no more talk of Catalina—ever."

"Ah, so she did tell you," she said. "I told her to let it be our secret, but she told you, didn't she?"

He seized her arms. "You knew?" he said gratingly. "You knew her background and you didn't tell me?"

"Cameron, I think you love her. I know she loves you."

"No," he shouted. "And I'll hear no more."

"Cameron, she is Catalina. If she were really Osa's daughter, she would be no more than Catalina. Think. Does it really make a difference?"

He jerked away and left her.

It took four pack mules to bring down Bowen's gold. Lucky, when he saw it, said, "Well, I'll be dogged."

Bowen spent some time with everyone he could find who had witnessed Craw Maddock's act of shooting down an unarmed man in Osa's cantina, coaxing those few who could write into giving an account of the affair with proper witness to their signatures on the statements, writing out the affidavits of others and having people who could sign their names witness the X's. There wasn't much law in the territory, but Bowen didn't want to have any trouble with what there was. He realized that the deaths of Wilson and his four men had been witnessed only by those who were intimately involved, but nevertheless, he made up formal affidavits for all three Lockharts and Lucky, stating Wilson's reasons for first sending one of his hired hands into Dos Caballos and then coming himself to finish the job of putting the competition out of business.

Cameron, during the chore of bringing down Bowen's gold, was not overly talkative. Since, to his doubt, his sister was intent on marrying Lucky Smith and staying in the American West, and since Lucky wasn't a bad sort, if a bit rustic, he spoke when he was spoken to and answered Lucky's interested questions about what kind of little girl Cara had been, and about their life in Scotland.

Lucky was too dazed at his fortune in winning Cara, too concerned about how he was going to make her a life of the sort she deserved, to notice that Cameron was often moody and withdrawn. In a perfect world, Lucky couldn't imagine anyone being unhappy.

Bowen managed to delay the departure date of the coach by a few days by winning sympathy for the wounded man. Actually the wound was healing nicely, having been only in soft flesh. Cara's attentions kept it from going septic, and it was she who finally told Bowen that he could quit malingering and get ready to go so that she could have a proper wedding, with a minister, in Socorro.

An air of change was hanging over Dos Caballos, where change was usually nothing more than the passing of one of the older residents by natural means, for there was unusual activity at the cantina. Cameron Lockhart was not the only man in Dos Caballos who was experiencing the agonies of the damned. Osa Carranza was in the process of abandoning more than a place he loved, more than his home. He was, and there were times when he looked heavenward and beseeched the blessed Virgin, going to leave behind him the work of his father and his grandfather, leave a tradition, leave the only watering spot in the Fray Cristobals in the hands of a non-Carranza for the first time in a hundred years. That he had to do it was beyond question, for, women being women, Catalina had forced the issue by going morose and pale and silent on him. He had, after all, been promising her great things since she was old enough to understand, and he figured that her malaise was her way of telling him that the time had come.

Well, she was just a few weeks short of eighteen years, and her market value as a bride would slowly begin to diminish if he kept putting off the trip to San Francisco. He dug out all the letters he'd exchanged with his cousins in San Francisco, read them over to reassure himself that he and his daughter would, after all, be welcome, smiled when he read the old but warm invitations and assurances that, yes, for a beautiful girl of Carranza blood there would be a good match available with a gentleman of blood and worth.

With some stern looks from Zelma, Mack Clemmons had agreed to take over the cantina and run it in Osa's tradition until Osa had Catalina safely married. Then Osa would come back, and it was that thought, more than any other, that led to Osa's agony, for to picture himself here, and Catalina there, to think of the Dos Caballos Cantina without the songs and the smiles of his daughter was a sadness so great that tears often wet Osa's cheeks.

But the day came.

Osa was saddened further when he saw that the interest in taking the coach down to Socorro had faded since that night of the great gala in the cantina when, it seemed, there had been a spirit-induced enthusiasm that had had Lucky turning down folks because the coach was already full. There were only three paying customers, since, of course, the co-owner and his daughter rode free.

Osa and Catalina's belongings, mostly the fine clothes that Osa had been buying one or two pieces at a time for the past five years, made the top of the stage look lumpy and uneven. Cameron Lockhart was sitting in the driver's box. Lucky helped Catalina and Cara into the coach. Osa and Bowen sat facing backward. The two girls faced forward, and Catalina was putting on a fine show, giggling and laughing as if she actually felt the excitement she was pretending.

"The great adventure begins, eh, Osa?" Bowen asked. "Don't look so blasted miserable."

"You can talk," Osa said. "You are not leaving two businesses in the hands of . . ." He paused.

"I wouldn't worry," Bowen said. "Mack seems to be an honest fellow, and I feel that our young Lucky is going to become a power in this godforsaken land." At that Cara beamed.

"In fact," Bowen said, "I've a proposition for you, my hairy friend. My future son-in-law and I are going to make an offer for the stage line owned by the late Mr. Wilson, and I'm sure that an astute businessman such as yourself would not want to miss such an opportunity. As it happens, we have a one-quarter share that is available, so don't spend all your money in San Francisco."

Osa groaned.

The stage jerked into motion with a "Hi-yah" from Lucky. Both Osa and Catalina shed a few tears, for different reasons, as Dos Caballos faded into the distance.

The trip was easy and uneventful for the first few miles. Lucky, who hadn't thought about Nana and his spirit man for some time, grew more alert when they entered the little valley where Nana had once ambushed the coach, but wheels rolled on, throwing sand, and the stage rocked along on its leather bed, and Cameron sat morosely atop the coach in silence. Lucky was wondering if he could get away with taking Bowen's fare money to buy a new suit to wear during the wedding ceremony. Then the road began to corkscrew up the side of the canyon wall and the horses puffed and labored and Lucky stopped to let them blow at the top.

Late in the day, the road wound down to a brushy flat and arrowed toward another rocky ridge about two miles away. They'd make the Rio Grande in time to set up camp in daylight. Lucky was getting a little weary, what with having wrestled with six sets of reins for nine hours. Cameron was dozing. He was still dozing when an Apache arrow whizzed past his head and narrowly missed Lucky's nose. Then the air was filled with the war cries of the Chiricahua.

They came boiling out of the brush. Lucky wondered how thirty or so young Apache warriors and horses could have been so easily concealed. They were on both sides of the coach, but they were not closing. After the initial rush from concealment they paced the slow-moving vehicle at a distance of almost a hundred years.

Cameron jerked and reached for Lucky's rifle. "Hold on," Lucky said.

He, himself, had heard Nana make a vow to the old chief, Orejas de Lobo, while the chief lay dying. Fortunately for them, the man who was most instrumental in that vow was inside the coach.

"Osa," Lucky yelled, "stick your head out the door so that they can see you."

Osa poked his head out. Nana was leading the single file of warriors on the south side of the coach. "Nana," Osa yelled, "my friend. It is I, Osa Carranza."

The now silent Apache rode on, Nana not turning his head. "Well," Lucky said, "so much for vows."

"Nana," Osa called out. "I also have my daughter aboard. On the vow of your father and your grandfather, let there be peace."

"Can we not make a run for it?" Cameron asked, holding the rifle so tightly that his knuckles were white.

"These horses have been pulling for nine hours," Lucky said. "They wouldn't last long."

For two miles the Apache paced the coach, silent, not even looking at it. Nana, in the regalia of a chief, rode with his back straight, his eyes ahead. Inside the coach, Bowen was seeing to the loads of his Sharps and his dueling pistols.

"They will not harm us," Osa said. "For I have too long been a friend of the Apache."

"Let me have one of your pistols," Cara said, reaching out a hand. Bowen gave her a pistol, placed powder and shot where both could reach it.

"You do know how to shoot?" Bowen asked.

"Yes. Actually I'm a more accurate shot than Cameron, much to his dismay," she said.

"We will not have to shoot," Osa said, but he was beginning to look a bit doubtful. The old chief was dead. Had the old vows died with him?

"The pinch is going to come when we enter the mouth of that canyon up ahead," Lucky said. "It narrows down there, and they'll be riding up above us, so they can shoot down on us and have brush and rocks for cover."

Sure enough, the Apache began to climb the slopes on either side, increasing their speed and disappearing among brush and boulders.

"Perhaps we should turn back," Cameron said.

"We're nine hours from Dos Caballos," Lucky said, thinking that the suggestion required no other comment. "Be ready. If they're going to do anything, they'll do it here. If they start shooting arrows at us, I'm going to make a run for it to get through the canyon. There's a spot on the other end where we can fort up behind some rocks."

Cameron was looking up at the arid walls of the canyon. Once he thought he saw motion, but he couldn't be sure. His hands were tense on the rifle. Lucky had his Navy Colt on the seat beside him, ready for action.

"What if they shoot the horses?" Cameron asked.

"I doubt it. Horses are too valuable. There are over thirty of them, and three of us with guns. If Nana's spirit man wants the coach bad enough to forget a vow to old Orejas de Lobo, then he knows he can take it. He'll lose a few men, but that won't stop him if he's really got his mind set on it."

"I take it that there's quite a good likelihood that we'll die here," Cameron said.

"Well, I'm going to resist the idea as much as possible," Lucky said.

Cameron's impulse was to lean down and shout into the window, to tell Catalina that he loved her. He didn't feel at all excited about the possibility of dying with an Apache arrow in his throat, but somehow he knew he'd feel better when he drew his last breath if he had spoken the truth to Catalina. The impulse, however, was not strong enough to overcome his background and his common sense. If he told Catalina he loved her, after all, and they lived, then he'd be honor-bound to take her back to Scotland with him, and he was still not ready to face the knowledge that he'd be taking the daughter of a Mexican whore into the bosom of his mother's family.

"Something moved up there," Cameron said, and the words were hardly out of his mouth when a volley of arrows whizzed down. They thunked into the sides of the coach and sped past the two men in the driver's box. One went in the open window and buried its head in the floorboard between Osa's feet.

"Madre de Dios," Osa whispered.

Lucky spanked the backs of the horses with the reins, cracked his whip, yelled out. The startled horses leapt into motion. The stage bucked and swayed, tossing about those inside. Bowen tried to draw a bead on a warrior in the rocks above, but the Indian ducked down after sending an arrow winging. The coach sped on in a cloud of dust. Froth formed around the bits in the mouths of the already tired horses. Lucky managed to snap off one shot but almost lost the reins, then decided to leave the shooting to Cameron. Cameron took Lucky's Colt and emptied it, doing no damage but causing a couple of warriors to duck. Then the Apache were back on their horses, weaving through the boulders on the sloping hills on either side, almost keeping pace with the coach. It was, Lucky estimated, about another half mile to the point where the canyon opened out into a field of huge, fallen boulders where they could find cover and have a clear field of fire.

"Dadgum," Lucky said. "They're going to beat us to it."

Indeed, Nana was leading a group of the Apache down from the slope onto the road. Once on the road, they bent low over the necks of their ponies and outdistanced the laboring team. The road straightened. A quarter mile ahead, Lucky could see that Nana and his warriors had taken up positions behind the very boulders he'd hoped would offer the coach and its passengers protection.

Osa stuck his head out of the window and yelled, "We must give them the coach, Lucky."

"You gonna give them Catalina and Cara, too?" Lucky yelled back.

Osa ducked back, thunderstruck. He hadn't thought of that. He knew how the Apache treated captured women.

"Would they do that?" Cara asked. "Wouldn't they be satisfied with the coach?"

Osa was facing grim reality, and it frightened the hell out of him. "Nana has broken the vow," he said. "If he will break a vow to his dying father, he will do anything."

"Look," Cara said, her blue eyes wide, frightened, looking at her father. "I'm not much for this death-before-dishonor thing that I've read about. Don't anyone tell me to save the last bullet for myself."

"No one's going to tell you that," Bowen said, but he, too, was frightened for his daughter.

Lucky pulled the horses back into a walk. He had to have time to think. He'd outdistanced most of the Apache warriors who were still riding through the brush and boulders on the slopes. No need to rush headlong into the range of Nana and his warriors ahead. He turned his head as the stage shifted on its bed, saw Bowen clambering atop. Lucky nodded, then saw Bowen put his Sharps down and start opening one of the bags. The Apache who had been left behind were slowly coming back within arrow range.

"Dadgum," Lucky said, thinking that Bowen had gone crazy under the strain, because the Scot was dropping his pants to reveal long red underwear, and then he buckled on his kilt, drew his tunic on over his shirt, and reached for the bagpipes.

"Bowen," Lucky said mildly, "I think, really, that the rifle would be more effective."

The pipes hummed, then a blast of sound that carried over the slow clip-clop of the hooves of six horses burst into the canyon, reverberating from the slopes. Bowen was standing erect atop the coach, feet planted among the bags, his red hair blowing in the slight breeze, piping for all he was worth.

Nana had been relaxing behind a boulder, letting others keep watch on the advancing stage. When he heard what seemed to be the dying wail of a dozen pumas, or the protest of lost souls, he leapt to his feet.

On the slope, a horse reared and threw its rider. The Apache slid, then tumbled, and came to rest near the road against a rock. One warrior gave a startled cry and jerked his horse to a stop. Others, after a frozen pause, turned their horses and went the other way.

"I'll be dadgummed," Lucky said. He saw the possibilities immediately. He let the horses walk on slowly toward the places of concealment of Nana and the group of Apache warriors. "Give it to 'em, Bowen," he whispered, and he grinned, because at that moment three warriors broke the cover of the boulders and sped away, whooping as if the devil himself was after them.

Just out of arrow range, Lucky pulled the coach to a stop. He stood. "Nana!" he yelled. "You, Nana!"

Nana, almost alone now, stepped up onto a boulder and posed, hands across his chest. He hoped that the white eyes were too far away to see that his own eyes were just a little wide.

Bowen stopped piping.

"Nana," Lucky shouted, "we have big medicine. We have the voices of your ancestors, wailing sorrow because you, a chief, seed of their loins, have broken your vow."

He nodded to Bowen and the pipes wailed. He hid a grin when he saw Nana take a step back and almost fall off the boulder.

"The spirit of your father, the great chief Orejas de Lobo, grieves," Lucky thundered, and Bowen punctuated the statement with a particularly tortured and unmelodic burst of sound.

"The spirits say, 'Does a vow mean nothing to the son of the great chief, Orejas de Lobo?' " Lucky shouted.

"The ghost of my father does not ride the shining wickiup on wheels," Nana shouted back.

"You hear his voice, and the voice of great Apache warriors who mourn the breaking of a vow," Lucky said, and Bowen played.

Nana, overcome, fell to his knees and began to chant to ward off evil spirits and, hopefully, the angry spirit of his father. Lucky sat down. "Keep playing, Bowen," he said, getting the horses into motion.

"When you get even with him, stop," Bowen said.

"Let's not push our luck," Lucky said.

"Stop, I say." Bowen panted, just a bit out of breath, thinking that maybe he'd have to cut down on the Scotch a bit and get back into shape if he was going to have to pipe the coach through on each trip up or down the hill.

Lucky stopped the coach. Nana was still kneeling, appealing to his Apache spirits.

"Nana," Bowen said, "you have heard the displeasure of the spirits of your dead ancestors. Now there's no harm done, is there? No one's hurt. The vow has been bent a little but not broken."

Nana stopped chanting and looked down, beginning to have a little hope. "The vow has not been broken," he said. He shrugged. "A bit of fun. High-spirited warriors, that's all."

"But the spirits were angry," Bowen said, giving one wail on the pipes that made Nana cringe.

"I now renew the vow," Nana said, standing and holding up one hand. "I, Nana, chief of the Chiricahua, vow never-ending peace between Chiricahua and Dos Caballos."

"We vow our friendship for Nana and the Chiricahua," Lucky said. "But the coach is going to be going up and down the hill every now and then. Do we have to bring along the spirits of your ancestors in the medicine bag each time to be sure that Nana's spirit man does not still hunger for the shining wickiup on wheels?"

Nana raised his hand. "I have spoken with my spirit man. He hears the voices of the dead."

"*Adios*, Nana," Lucky said, clucking at the horses.

Nana stood on the boulder for a long, long time. Bowen looking back, decided to give it one more go for good measure, and burst into a spirited rendition of "The Bluebells of Scotland." He grinned around the mouthpiece when Nana leapt from the boulder directly onto the back of his horse and left the vicinity on the gallop.

Years later, as a mature war leader of the Chiricahua, Nana would remember his encounter with the spirits of his ancestors with some doubt.

Chapter Fifteen

"I don't see that it makes a helluva lot of difference," Bowen said. "Catholic, Episcopalian, Presbyterian, each as bloody as the other, fighting as if they weren't supposed to be working the same side of the street of salvation."

Cara, with a single-mindedness that had left Bowen and Lucky breathless, had been whirling around Socorro making preparations for the union of one Cara Lockhart and one Christopher, alias Lucky, Smith. Now, after an eventful day, the three of them were at table in a boardinghouse that served excellent beef stew.

"This isn't Scotland," Cara said. "Here, at least, religion isn't being used as an excuse to murder one's fellows."

"So?" Bowen said. "I vote for the church. At least we'll have a roof over our heads and some semblance of civilized trappings."

The Church of San Miguel was, of course, Catholic, presided over by an aging priest who spoke Spanish-accented English and smiled benignly.

"No damned Presbyterians here," Bowen grunted. "No Whiskeypalians, either."

"There is a sort of itinerant Methodist minister," Cara said. "They call them circuit riders. He's here now, as a matter of fact. At least he's Protestant.''

"What do you think, Lucky?" Bowen asked.

Lucky, still not believing that the creamy, colorful beauty of this girl was soon to be his, said, "Huh?"

"I said, does it make a damn to you where and under what Christian sect you're united in holy matrimony?" Bowen rolled his eyes. "Good Lord, man, we've got business to conduct."

"No, no," Lucky said. "Whatever Cara wants."

"I want to go and speak with the Methodist minister," Cara said firmly.

"It's almost dark," Bowen mumbled.

"Oh, there's time enough," Lucky said.

He threw out his chest and strutted a little as he went out of the dining room with Cara clinging to his manly arm.

There were bits of green in Socorro. The little town sat in a rather pretty valley, mountains rising abruptly to one side, the Rio Grande making its way serenely past. The population was mainly Hispanic. Anglos were beginning to drift into the territory now that there was a semblance of peace with the Navajo and Apache, but the residents of Socorro did not object at all to the presence of a small number of troops stationed there.

The federal troops, when they were not flaring off on false alarms regarding the invading forces of Confederate forces from Texas, were the only law in the area, and it was to the commanding officer, a captain, that Bowen delivered his written statement and affidavits, with his oral explanation of what he felt were the timely deaths of Wilson and his hirelings. The captain, looking forward hopefully to a chance at glory in a meeting with the Confederates, glanced perfunctorily at the papers, threw them aside, and said, "Sounds as if justice was served, Major Bowen." Thus it was that Bowen had introduced himself. He hoped that the captain would keep his mouth shut, for he had told no one that he'd held that rank in Victoria's army.

"We could use a man of your experience," the captain said. "I have the authority to muster you in at the rank of captain."

"Nice of you," Bowen said noncommittally, taking his leave.

* * *

The Reverend Andrew W. Foote had built his brush arbor on the northern outskirts of town on a shady flat near the river. A ragged army tent was set up, a fire smoldering in front of it, a line strung between two trees with drying clothes to the rear. A friendly-faced woman of indeterminate years sat in a camp chair near the tent.

"Welcome, welcome," she said when Lucky and Cara walked up. "I'm Elmira Foote."

Lucky introduced Cara, then himself, and then fell silent. Cara stated her desire to get married, bringing a smile to the face of the minister's wife. "I'm sure the mister will be pleased to accommodate you."

"Tomorrow morning," Cara said definitely.

"Ah, where will it happen?" Lucky asked.

"Nothing like being close to God in the open air," Mrs. Foote said.

"Here?" Lucky asked.

"I think it's lovely," Cara said.

"You're Methodist, dearie?" Mrs. Foote asked.

"Actually, Presbyterian."

"Ah," Mrs. Foote said. "I will warn you, then, that the mister tends to be a bit hard-shelled in such matters. He'll marry you, but I warrant he'll do a little sermonizing about true religion and the proper church. If he's full of beans, he might jump down your throat and dance a jig on your gizzard and dare your heart to beat one sinful Presbyterian beat."

Cara laughed. "Whatever it takes," she said, clutching Lucky's arm.

Actually it was a rather lovely ceremony. As usual, Bowen was splendid in his tartans as he gave the bride away. Cameron was moody and silent. Catalina, in white, was radiant as bridesmaid. Osa was still wondering if Mack Clemmons was filling the glasses too full or being careless with the inventory. The Reverend Foote controlled himself admirably, deviating from the Protestant ceremony only twice to denounce Papists, deluded Baptists, Episcopalians, and *other* deviant sects, and when Lucky finally lifted Cara's veil and kissed her, the waters of the Rio Grande chuckled happily, the early-morning sun brightened, and songbirds broke out into melody.

Cameron waited until after the wedding breakfast to put a pall on the day by announcing that he had passage on the morning stage to El Paso, that he planned to take ship in New Orleans after taking the southern route. To add to that blow, Osa said that he and Catalina would be on the way in the opposite direction on the morrow as well.

Bowen said to Lucky, "Son, ye'll have to rush the honeymoon, for Wilson died without heirs, and the stage line from Santa Fe to El Paso is up for grabs."

Lucky had one minute alone with his new bride, in the big, airy room that overlooked a courtyard that was well watered and sported roses. Then Cara said, "Darling, I must see Cameron," and was gone.

Cameron was in his room. He'd been lying down when Cara knocked, and his hair was tousled and his shirt pulled out of his trousers when he opened the door.

Cameron smiled. "Have you had a falling-out so soon?"

"Not at all, ninny," she said. She sat, arranged her skirts, looked at him, and burst into tears.

"Here, here," he said. "Look, you're not sorry, are you? So soon?"

"No," she said, sobbing. "No, I'm very, very happy."

"That is happy?" he asked teasingly, lifting her chin with his finger.

"Oh, Cameron, I'm going to miss you so."

He turned away, felt his own eyes sting. "I'm so glad you came," he said. "I wanted to see you alone for a few minutes before—before I leave."

"You don't have to go," she said, beginning to control the quick burst of weeping.

He faced her and wiped a tear with the back of his hand. "I do. I do, indeed."

Cara was silent for a moment, thinking. She decided that it had to be said. "You're leaving more than a sister behind, you know."

"I? Leaving you? It seems to me that you are the one who chose to stay. If I had thought for one minute that I'd lose you here, I never would have left Scotland."

"You're ignoring the implication of my statement," she said. "I've found happiness here. So could you."

"I will not speak of that," he said, turning his back again.

"Then I will," she said firmly. "You're being utterly boorish, Cameron. I love you and I respect you, but you are. First of all, you're

going on an assumption of fact that might be erroneous. I've been thinking about it. How does anyone know that Catalina's mother was a—a
woman of ill-repute? Because the Apache said so? What if her mother
was taken from a brothel? Consider this. In a small village there is an
attack by the Indians. People would, quite naturally, run for cover.
What if some very respectable woman, being out on the street at the
time, found the only source of cover to be the brothel?"

"Osa told Lucky, in Catalina's hearing," Cameron said. "He must
have known."

"And did that knowledge make Osa love Catalina any less? Is Osa
more of a man than you, my Scottish laird?"

"You simply don't understand."

"Oh, I think I do. I think my brother views the world with a double
standard."

"Perhaps."

"You are willing to call Catalina's mother whore without knowing
the true facts. What name would you apply to our own mother?"

"Easy," Cameron said, turning to face her, his face set in hard lines.

"Oh, you know, as well as I, that it is true. You think that I have forgotten, for I was quite young, the time we entered her room quietly—
and she was still living with father, when he was at home—to see her
doing something neither of us quite understood at the time. You, as well
as I, have contrived not to notice other things since. And yet wasn't she
doing the same thing, if without overt monetary gain, that Catalina's
mother did?"

"I don't like that kind of talk," Cameron said.

"Yet it is not Catalina who has sinned," Cara said. "Did you see her
today, in white? Cameron, I know that girl. I have seen her smile and
flirt, but she is as untouched as a desert flower never seen by human
eyes. She . . . well, I would be happy to call her sister, and I think
you're being a proper prig."

"I will hear no more of this," Cameron said, slamming out of his own
room.

But he was tearful and gentle when he embraced Cara the next morning, shortly after dawn. "Please come back to visit us," she whispered.

"Yes, when things are in order at home," he said. He turned to Bowen,
clasped hands. Bowen put his hands on his shoulders and smiled.

"I have a son of whom I can be rightly proud," Bowen said.

"I hope you can come back sometime," Lucky said, shaking Cameron's hand.

Cara was not weeping as the stage jerked away and sped out of town. Then there was another leave-taking, and there were tears from both girls as Cara and Catalina said farewell.

"Find the finest, most handsome, richest young man in San Francisco," Cara whispered, so that the men couldn't hear. "Remember, just lower your head, smile, and blink your eyes through those wonderful lashes."

"I will," Catalina said with a sob.

"Well, my children," Bowen said after honking into a handkerchief, "I would, if I could, see you honeymooning in Paris, or in London at the worst, but since we're a bit of a jaunt from either place, I'll give you two days before we put this young man to work."

What happened in the pleasant, airy room in the boardinghouse would always be Lucky and Cara's secret. What Bowen did was to visit the lawyer, Sykes, and begin inquiries as to the law regarding the property of a man who had died without a proper will and with no known heirs. It was to be a long, drawn-out affair, with some governmental entity coming into Wilson's property if legitimate heirs could not be discovered. The process, Sykes said, would take years, perhaps.

"Would not the territory, or the United States, or any discovered heirs be as content with money as with a stagecoach line that would in all probability be defunct by the time things are settled?" Bowen asked.

"I could make certain inquiries," Sykes said. "I'm sure that those in the territorial government would rather have a functioning stage line and money in the bank than the remnants of a stage line some years from now."

Next Bowen turned his attentions toward finding a love nest for the newlyweds and happened upon a splendid bargain in a Spanish casa with rambling rooms, tall adobe walls, and lovely courtyards. It was to be his wedding present. However, he dined alone and did not see hide nor hair of his daughter or son-in-law until the two-day interval he had set down had expired.

Lucky came out of his daze when Bowen started telling him that the local justice of the peace had issued a preliminary opinion that the properties of one Chunk Wilson might just be legally available, under a territorial trusteeship, to owners with the experience and financial means to keep the stages running.

"I have the means, and you have the experience, being the longtime owner of the Dos Caballos Stage Company," Bowen said.

Cara fell in love with the casa immediately, found two Spanish women to help her, and dived into an orgy of cleaning and polishing. Bowen had a cozy suite of rooms in one wing of the house.

So much had happened, so soon. She had not been in Socorro and married for a week, and already she had a lovely house, with hardworking, amiable servants, a husband who adored her, and the knowledge that her husband and her father were going to be in business together. Her only regret was that she had not been able to convince Cameron that he was so wrong in leaving without declaring his true feelings for Catalina. She was beginning to pick up some Spanish and found it to be a musical, beautiful language. She told Lucky and Bowen that she was going to give a huge party, and that she would invite the best of Socorro society. Bowen added a few names to the list, people who would be helpful, he felt, in securing the sale of Wilson's holdings to the Dos Caballos Stage Company.

During preparations for the party Lucky kept getting underfoot. He had not, as yet, gotten his eyes full of Cara, and he followed her around with an awestruck expression.

"Lucky, for heaven's sake," Cara said, smiling fondly, "why don't you go get Father and go hunting or something?"

"I'd rather go hunting with you," Lucky said, winking. "If he got his clothing ripped off, he wouldn't be nearly as interesting."

"You are a terrible man," she said, but she was smiling as he bent to kiss her, and then it was she who had to remember her work. "Go. Get out of here. Stop tempting me."

"Only if you promise to let Rosa and Chica do the hard work, so as not to tire yourself out, if you know what I mean," Lucky said.

"I know full well what you mean," she said.

So, some timeless period later, with the heat of the day hung over Socorro and the Hispanic population showing good, Latin common sense in siesta, when she heard footsteps, she assumed it was Lucky.

"I thought I had you out from underfoot," she said playfully, without turning.

"Is that a way to greet a returning brother?"

At the sound of the voice she whirled. "Cameron, oh, Cameron," she cried, rushing to throw herself into his arms.

"You'll get all dusty," he said.

He was showing travel signs, his clothing sweated through, the smell of horse about him, dust coating him finely.

"I am so happy to see you," she said, kissing him. And then she pushed herself away and her face went stern. "Damn you—"

"I'll wash your mouth out with soap," he said.

"That's not your affair. I am a proper married woman, and I think my husband would approve of a bit of profanity applied to you."

"Don't be harsh."

"I feel harsh," she said. "Why did you go? Here you are back, and now it's too late."

"Perhaps not," he said.

"But it is. She's gone." She looked into his face, saw a determination there that she'd never seen.

"You *have* come to your senses," she said, smiling.

"I was halfway to El Paso," he said. "The stage was full, nine people inside. One of them was a fat lady, and she sat next to me. She made a very good pillow when the road was smooth enough to catch a nap."

"You're talking, but you're not saying anything," she said, taking his hand and leading him toward the kitchen.

"I kept seeing her face," he said. He did not add that he kept seeing Catalina's face, and other parts of her, those parts he had loved and admired on the banks of a small, clear creek far up in the Fray Cristobals. "I kept remembering what you'd said. Perhaps the Apache who told Osa about the Mexican woman were wrong."

"It doesn't matter," she said, pouring water and handing it to him. He drank deeply.

"No," he said. He grinned. "I've read accounts of the conquest of Mexico. The Indians showered the conquistadores with presents, gold, and women. The half-breed sons of the conquistadores helped in the conquest of Peru, did you know that?"

"I didn't, and I don't see the relevance."

"All Mexicans have the blood of the conquistadores in them," he said. "We trace our ancestory back to the original Caledonii. And in doing so we're kidding ourselves, because that original Scot blood was diluted by wave after wave of peoples. Hell, if we're Scot, then Catalina is pure Spanish aristocrat, descendant of the conquistadores, maybe even old Lord Cortés himself, with a bloodline going back as far as ours."

"If you have to rationalize it, that's fine, whatever it takes," she said. "But I think I remember reading that Cortés was a poor man in Spain."

"As a matter of fact, his parents were minor aristocrats, of little wealth but much honor, just as our ancestors were."

"Those who weren't smugglers." Cara giggled. She took the glass from his hand and put it down. "You're going after her, aren't you?"

"Yes."

"Osa might shoot you."

"He doesn't carry a gun."

"He might be carrying that cedar shillelagh."

"Then I'll just have to take my chances."

In fact, he had already figured out how he would convince Osa. If, after he pressed his suit and asked for Catalina's hand, Osa still held out for a husband of Spanish blood, he would simply confess that he, Laird Cameron Lockhart, had dishonored Osa's daughter and, having stolen her purity, now insisted on restoring her good name through marriage. If it became necessary to make that statement, he would, of course, stand far away, out of reach of Osa and Osa's club.

"I'm so proud of you," Cara said.

"I'm not so proud of myself, but I'll do my best to make up for it," he said. "How is your supply of horses? The one I bought is quite spent."

"For the young Lochinvar in pursuit of his lady love, there will be the finest horse in Socorro," she said. "We'll see to it as soon as Lucky and Father get back from hunting, or from the saloon, whatever the case may be."

"Now," he said.

"This minute?"

"A coach averages five and a half miles an hour. It's been days."

"All right."

157

She did manage to push a chunk of leftover venison into his hand as he mounted. He turned to wave, chewing at the same time, and then he was gone. She went back into the casa smiling happily.

Chapter Sixteen

Osa was sure that the luck that had previously cursed his partner had followed him. From the time he had boarded a westbound stage in Socorro, Lucky's luck had haunted him. He missed the step at the first way station and barked his shin. Before the end of the first day, the coach threw a wheel on the fly, and although it didn't overturn, the tilting, dusty, scratching stop threw a woman who must have weighed three hundred pounds atop him and wrenched his back. The various drivers knew every rut, pothole, and rock in New Mexico. Lack of fresh horses, something unheard of in the days of Butterworth Overland, stranded the coach for a full day and on into the next morning.

He did not realize until later that what he thought was bad luck was actually good luck or the *bueno Dio* looking out for him.

He had wrangled a seat atop, to get some fresh air and to get away from the three-hundred-pound woman, who wanted to flirt, seeing potential husband material in a mature man with a young daughter. He was seated facing backward. The stage was proceeding west at a slow lope. He saw a small dust cloud, not sure what it was at first, as he looked backward through the coach's own dust cloud.

"There is a rider overtaking us," he told the driver and the shotgun.

"Keep an eye on 'im," the driver said, looking over his shoulder.

"He is coming up fast," Osa said a few minutes later.

"You got a good seat," the driver said, "take this rifle. Cain't tell what kind of buzzard you'll run into out here."

Osa took the rifle. The rider came pounding up through the cloud of dust.

"If he's aiming to rob us, he's pretty dumb," the shotgun said. "Shoulda laid in wait up in them hills, where we have to slow to a walk."

"If he looks at you cross-eyed," the driver said to Osa, "shoot his ass."

Osa was in a mood where shooting someone's ass might just give him some satisfaction. He cocked the rifle and raised it to his shoulder, eyed down the barrel, and saw a familiar face.

"Don't shoot, Osa," Cameron yelled, bringing the horse up off the rear wheel. "Tell them to stop the stage."

"It is a friend," Osa said. "He is not out to rob. Please stop."

"We don't stop for nothing," the driver said.

"You will stop for this," Osa said, putting the muzzle of the rifle in the driver's back.

"I stop for that," the driver said, pulling on the reins.

Catalina looked out the window and saw a dusty, sweaty man who had Cameron's face. When he saw her, he smiled and yelled, "I'm taking you back, Catalina."

"What's this?" Osa shouted.

"I love your daughter, Osa," Cameron yelled as the stage came to a halt. "I want to marry her."

"Young love in the purple sage," the driver said with a moan. "Say, Mr. Carranza, you wanna take that gun out of my back?"

"Yes?" Cameron asked Catalina. "Will you say yes?"

Catalina leaned far out and looked up at her father, who sighed. "Yes," she shouted.

"Osa, is that all right with you?" Cameron asked. "I would have been a bit more formal, and I would have spoken to you first, but, well, you see the circumstances. I can't follow this stagecoach forever."

Osa rolled out a few choice Mexican oaths.

"What?" Cameron said. "My Spanish is very poor. I didn't get that."

"He said," Catalina said, "why in the hell didn't you speak up before he had to suffer the tortures of the damned on this useless journey? He said if you had spoken before, he would not—"

"I can speak for myself," Osa shouted. "If you had spoken before, I would not have had to ride through the badlands on a vehicle invented by the devil. I would not have had to leave my cantina in the hands of a storekeeper."

"I'm sorry, Osa," Cameron said. "May I have the honor of your daughter's hand in marriage?"

"Say yes," Catalina said.

"Say yes," the driver said, "so we can get going."

"Say yes," the fat lady said. "It's so romantic."

"Yes," Osa shouted. "Yes, yes, yes. Let us go on to the next station so that we can be tortured with beans not properly cooked, a bed not fit for a sow, and then a ride back home."

The kindly priest of the Church of San Miguel said kindly that he could not join in marriage a good Catholic, Catalina, and a Presbyterian, Cameron. The Reverend Andrew Foote said he would but inserted into his ceremony some choice, but diplomatic, remarks about the delusions of Papists and Presbyterians.

Then, after a long, quiet time during which the Dos Caballos Stage Company expanded rapidly, the Laird and Lady Lockhart boarded a Dos Caballos Company stage. This time the tears of parting were not sad but bittersweet.